CHILDREN'S
CLASSICS
TO READ ALOUD

Selected by Edward Blishen

Kingfisher
NEW YORK

KINGFISHER
Larousse, Kingfisher, Chambers Inc.
95 Madison Avenue,
New York, New York 10016

First American edition in hardcover, 1992
First American edition in paperback, 1995

2 4 6 8 10 9 7 5 3 1

Library of Congress Cataloging-in-Publication Data
Children's classics to read aloud/
selected by Edward Blishen,
1st American ed.
p.   cm.
Summary A collection of excerpts from classics in children's literature, including "Tom
Sawyer," "The Secret Garden," and "Charlotte's Web."
1. Children's literature. [1. Literature—Collections.]
I. Blishen, Edward.
PZ5. C4356 1995
[Fic.]—dc20   94–26070 CIP AC

ISBN 1–85697–538–X

Designed by Caroline Johnson
Cover art by Yvonne Gilbert

CONTENTS

INTRODUCTION

The best books are made to be read aloud and to be shared with at least one other person. About this I have no doubt. I know it from my experience as a child, being read to; as a teacher and parent, reading aloud to children; and from my work as a writer. Hearing a book read aloud as well as possible is a great stimulant of the imagination, as well as being the best means of helping us to feel the shape of the language, its rhythms, the great richness of words, and the thrilling effect of the surprisingly right word in the surprisingly right place.

I am joined in this belief by many teachers and educators. You cannot, they say, overemphasize the importance of being read to as a major step toward literacy. Research with gifted children has shown that, despite differences in home circumstances, these children have one thing in common: throughout their school years, they were read to by their parents or other members of their families.

It is no exaggeration to say that, without the skill of reading, our children are unlikely to succeed in any area of study. To read aloud to children is not to encourage laziness. It is simply one of the best contributions parents can make toward their children's education, and one that will improve the children's own silent and private reading.

Sadly, mistakenly, many parents stop reading aloud when their children begin to read for themselves. But children enjoy being read to at all ages; and they will benefit enormously from having books read to them that are beyond their reading skills and that will introduce them to new worlds, as well as to new and more complex words and structures of language.

I felt all this as a teacher of literature: I felt it even more strongly as a parent. Books read by parents to children (or by children to parents) provide shared imaginative experiences. To me there is no other ingredient of family life to match this sharing of excitement and uncertainties ("How will the story end?") and the exchange of shared references ("Reminds me of *Tom Sawyer*, remember?").

The Stories

The main consideration I had in mind when choosing passages for this book was that each one had to be likely to entertain and interest adult and child alike. But the truth is that the mere fact that I was selecting extracts from classics of children's literature meant that this was so. A good children's book can be defined as one that does not delight only children.

Another consideration was that each passage should be an example of "classic" writing. When I was small, that word "classic" suggested leather-bound books, unread and perhaps unreadable, locked away in glass-fronted bookcases. That is not what I mean by "classic" here. I mean a book that has been read till the covers drop off, either by generations of children, or, in the case of more recent books, in such a way by a single generation (or two) that here, clearly, is a book of classic quality. *Charlotte's Web* was published as recently as 1952, but I haven't an ounce of doubt that children will still be reading it in the year 2052.

The problem was that there are scores of children's classics. How could I choose among them? What I've set out to do is, first to select passages or stories addressed to children of various ages from five years old and up. They are not grouped according to listening age, because I feel that the quality of the writing or the nature of the imagination at work makes each selection likely to be of interest to all ages. Only you as parents will know what your children are ready to hear, as well as what should be kept until they are older; and you will choose what to read accordingly. Second, I've tried to balance the various kinds of story, the comic and the dramatic, the domestic and the adventurous, the home-based and the exotic.

Finally, I've attempted to make sure that every extract is satisfying in itself. It may lead to a hunt for the book from which the extract was taken by readers who can't bear not to know what happened after that or, of course, before it. But if ever I leave readers clinging to the edge of a cliff by their fingertips, I've tried to make sure that this is not an entirely disagreeable position to be in. In the extract from *Moonfleet*, you'll notice, the audience *is* left at the top of a cliff, and they will certainly wonder what happened to John Trenchard and Elzevir Block when they got there: but the getting there ... that's a totally satisfying story in itself.

A Word about Reading Aloud

As someone who had first to acquire the skill in some rumbustious and highly critical classrooms, let me say that I don't think it should ever be done shyly. It should be done for all its worth. If you overdo it, your audience will soon say so. But you might discover you're underdoing it only when you find they've fallen asleep.

Readers-aloud should take their time: many of us go too fast – too fast, that is, for the ear, the mind, the imagination of the listener. Clarity is essential. There are of course passages that are best read at speed. It is no good reading some of the more thrilling passages from *The Hobbit* at a funereal pace. Other passages yield their true quality only when read deliberately, lingeringly. A good book dictates its own speed, as well as varying volumes of voice (not just for what the characters say, but for the narration itself). The more reading aloud we do, the more we're able to pick up those hints which, in a good story, are inbuilt.

I vividly remember mispronouncing the name of a Greek god as a young teacher reading aloud to a class of bright and scornful ten-year-olds; so on page 252 you will find a list of helpful definitions for old fashioned, or strange sounding words together with their pronunciations.

Finally, I wish you many happy hours of reading with your children. I hope you will have great pleasure in sharing the passages in this book, and will go on to discover and read together the classics from which they are taken.

Good reading!

Edward Blishen

UNDER THE HILL

from
THE HOBBIT
by
J. R. R. TOLKIEN

The Hobbit *is a sort of run-up to a huge, but not easily describable, trio of books that have the general title of* The Lord of the Rings. *In them, Tolkien (who lived from 1892 to 1973) invented a whole world: one in which goblins and elves and dwarves and wizards and dragons become strangely real and have adventures like episodes from some wonderful series of dreams and nightmares. In* The Hobbit, *the dwarves, led by Gandalf the wizard, have set off in quest of the dragon's treasure – taking with them that home-loving creature, Bilbo Baggins, the hobbit, who is a skilled burglar and has a sensible disinclination for*

adventure. Their horrific experience at the hands of the goblins, part of which is described in the passage below, is hair-raising enough: but it is nothing to what happens as they draw nearer to the final fantastic danger of their quest.

Gandalf knew that something unexpected might happen, and he hardly dared to hope that they would pass without fearful adventure over those great tall mountains with lonely peaks and valleys where no king ruled. They did not. All was well, until one day they met a thunderstorm – more than a thunderstorm, a thunderbattle. You know how terrific a really big thunderstorm can be down in the land and in a river valley; especially at times when two great thunderstorms meet and clash. More terrible still are thunder and lightning in the mountains at night, when storms come up from East and West and make war. The lightning splinters on the peaks, and rocks shiver, and great crashes split the air and go rolling and tumbling into every cave and hollow; and the darkness is filled with overwhelming noise and sudden light.

Bilbo had never seen or imagined anything of the kind. They were high up in a narrow place, with a dreadful fall into a dim valley at one side of them. There they were sheltering under a hanging rock for the night, and he lay beneath a blanket and shook from head to toe. When he peeped out in the lightning-flashes, he saw that across the valley the stone-giants were out, and were hurling rocks at one another for a game, and catching them, and tossing them down into the darkness, where they smashed among the trees far below, or splintered into little bits with a bang. Then came a wind and a rain, and the wind whipped the rain and the hail about in every direction, so that an overhanging rock was no protection at all. Soon they were getting drenched, and their ponies were standing with their heads down and their tails between their legs, and some of them were whinnying with fright. They could hear the giants guffawing and shouting all over the mountainsides.

"This won't do at all!" said Thorin. "If we don't get blown off, or drowned, or struck by lightning, we shall be picked up by some giant and kicked sky-high for a football."

"Well, if you know of anywhere better, take us there!" said Gandalf, who was feeling very grumpy, and was far from happy about the giants himself.

The end of their argument was that they sent Fili and Kili to look for a better shelter. They had very sharp eyes, and being the youngest of the dwarves by some fifty years, they usually got these sorts of jobs (when everybody could see that it was absolutely no use sending Bilbo). There is nothing like looking, if you want to find something (or so Thorin said to the young dwarves). You certainly usually find something, if you look, but it is not always quite the something you were after. So it proved on this occasion.

Soon Fili and Kili came crawling back, holding onto the rocks in the wind. "We have found a dry cave," they said, "not far round the next corner; and ponies and all could get inside."

"Have you *thoroughly* explored it?" said the wizard, who knew that caves up in the mountains were seldom unoccupied.

"Yes, yes!" they said, though everybody knew they could not have been long about it; they had come back too quick. "It isn't all that big, and it does not go far back."

That, of course, is the dangerous part about caves: you don't know how far they go back, sometimes, or where a passage behind may lead to, or what is waiting for you inside. But now Fili and Kili's news seemed good enough. So they all got up and prepared to move. The wind was howling and the thunder still growling, and they had a business getting themselves and their ponies along. Still it was not very far to go, and before long they came to a big rock standing out into the path. If you stepped behind, you found a low arch in the side of the mountain. There was just room to get the ponies through with a squeeze, when they had been unpacked and unsaddled. As they passed under the arch, it was good to hear the wind and the rain outside instead of all about them, and to feel safe from the giants and their rocks. But the wizard was taking no risks. He lit up his wand – as he did that day in Bilbo's dining room that seemed so long ago, if you remember – and by its light, they explored the cave from end to end.

It seemed quite a fair size, but not too large and mysterious. It had a dry floor and some comfortable nooks. At one end, there was room for the ponies; and there they stood (mighty glad of the change) steaming, and champing in their nosebags. Oin and Gloin wanted to light a fire at the door to dry their clothes, but Gandalf would not hear of it. So they spread out their wet things on the floor and got dry ones out of their bundles; then they made their blankets comfortable, got out their pipes, and blew smoke rings, which Gandalf turned into different colors and set dancing up by the roof to amuse them. They talked and talked, and forgot about the storm, and discussed what each would do with his share of the treasure (when they got it, which at the moment did not seem so impossible); and so they dropped off to sleep one by one. And that was the last time that they used the ponies, packages, baggages, tools, and paraphernalia that they had brought with them.

It turned out a good thing that night that they had brought little Bilbo with them, after all. For, somehow, he could not go to sleep for a long while; and when he did sleep, he had very nasty dreams. He dreamed that a crack in the wall at the back of the cave got bigger and bigger, and opened wider and wider, and he was very afraid but could not call out or do anything but lie and look. Then he dreamed that the floor of the cave was giving way, and he was slipping – beginning to fall down, down, goodness knows where to.

At that, he woke up with a horrible start and found that part of his dream was true. A crack had opened at the back of the cave and was already a wide passage. He was just in time to see the last of the ponies' tails disappearing into it. Of course, he gave a very loud yell, as loud a yell as a hobbit can give, which is surprising for their size.

Out jumped the goblins, big goblins, great ugly-looking goblins, lots of goblins, before you could say *rocks and blocks*. There were six to each dwarf, at least, and two even for Bilbo; and they were all grabbed and carried through the crack, before you could say *tinder and flint*. But not Gandalf. Bilbo's yell had done that much good. It had wakened him up wide in a splintered second, and when goblins came to grab him, there was a terrific flash like lightning in the cave, a smell like gunpowder, and several of them fell dead.

The crack closed with a snap, and Bilbo and the dwarves were on the wrong side of it! Where was Gandalf? Of that, neither they nor the goblins had any idea, and the goblins did not wait to find out. They seized Bilbo and the dwarves and hurried them along. It was deep, deep, dark, such as only goblins that have taken to living in the heart of the mountains can see through. The passages there were crossed and tangled in all directions, but the goblins knew their way, as well as you do to the nearest post office; and the way went down and down, and it was most horribly stuffy. The goblins were very rough, and pinched unmercifully, and chuckled and laughed in their horrible stony voices; and Bilbo was more unhappy even than when the troll had picked him up by his toes. He wished again and again for his nice, bright hobbit-hole. Not for the last time.

Now there came a glimmer of a red light before them. The goblins began to sing, or croak, keeping time with the flap of their flat feet on the stone, and shaking their prisoners as well.

Clap! Snap! the black crack!
Grip, grab! Pinch, nab!
And down down to Goblin-town
   You go, my lad!

Clash, crash! Crush, smash!
Hammer and tongs! Knocker and gongs!
Pound, pound, far underground!
   Ho, ho! my lad!

Swish, smack! Whip crack!
Batter and beat! Yammer and bleat!
Work, work! Nor dare to shirk,
While Goblins quaff, and Goblins laugh,
Round and round far underground
   Below, my lad!

It sounded truly terrifying. The walls echoed to the *clap, snap!* and the *crush, smash!* and to the ugly laughter of their *ho, ho! my lad!* The general meaning of the song was only too plain; for now the goblins took out whips and whipped them with a *swish, smack!*, and set them running as fast as they could in front of them; and more than one of the dwarves were already yammering and bleating like anything, when they stumbled into a big cavern.

It was lit by a great red fire in the middle, and by torches along the walls, and it was full of goblins. They all laughed and stamped and clapped their hands, when the dwarves (with poor little Bilbo at the back and nearest to the whips) came running in, while the goblin-drivers whooped and cracked their whips behind. The ponies were already there huddled in a corner; and there were all the baggages and packages lying broken open, and being rummaged by goblins, and smelt by goblins, and fingered by goblins, and quarreled over by goblins.

I am afraid that was the last they ever saw of those excellent little ponies, including a jolly, sturdy little white fellow that Elrond had lent to Gandalf, since his horse was not suitable for the mountain paths. For goblins eat horses and ponies and donkeys (and other much more dreadful things), and they are always hungry. Just now, however, the prisoners were thinking only of themselves. The goblins chained their hands behind their backs and linked them all together in a line, and dragged them to the far end of the cavern with little Bilbo tugging at the end of the row.

There in the shadows on a large flat stone sat a tremendous goblin with a huge head, and armed goblins were standing around him carrying the axes and the bent swords that they use. Now goblins are cruel, wicked, and bad-hearted. They make no beautiful things, but they make many clever ones. They can tunnel and mine as well as any but the most skilled dwarves, when they take the trouble, though they are usually untidy and dirty. Hammers, axes, swords, daggers, pick-axes, tongs, and also instruments of torture, they make very well, or get other people to make to their design, prisoners and slaves that have to work till they die for want of air and light. It is not unlikely that they invented some of the machines that have since troubled the world, especially the ingenious devices for killing large numbers of people at once, for wheels and explosions always delighted them, and also not working with their own hands more than they could help; but in those days and those wild parts, they had not advanced (as it is called) so far. They did not hate dwarves especially, no more than they hated everybody and everything, and particularly the orderly and prosperous; in some parts, wicked dwarves had even made alliances with them. But they had a special grudge against Thorin's people, because of the war which you have heard mentioned, but which does not come into this tale; and anyway goblins don't care who they catch, as long as it is done smart and secret, and the prisoners are not able to defend themselves.

"Who are these miserable persons?" said the Great Goblin.

"Dwarves, and this!" said one of the drivers, pulling at Bilbo's chain so that he fell forward onto his knees. "We found them sheltering in our Front Porch."

"What do you mean by it?" said the Great Goblin turning to Thorin. "Up to no good, I'll warrant! Spying on the private business of my people, I guess! Thieves, I shouldn't be surprised to learn! Murderers and friends of Elves, not unlikely! Come! What have you got to say?"

"Thorin the dwarf at your service!" he replied – it was merely a polite nothing. "Of the things which you suspect and imagine we had no idea at all. We sheltered from a storm in what seemed a convenient cave and unused; nothing was further from our thoughts than inconveniencing goblins in any way whatever." That was true enough!

"Um!" said the Great Goblin. "So you say! Might I ask what you were doing up in the mountains at all, and where you were coming from, and where you were going to? In fact, I should like to know all about you. Not that it will do you much good, Thorin Oakenshield, I know too much about your folk already; but let's have the truth, or I will prepare something particularly uncomfortable for you!"

"We were on a journey to visit our relatives, our nephews and nieces, and first, second, and third cousins, and the other descendants of our grandfathers, who live on the East side of these truly hospitable mountains," said Thorin, not quite knowing what to say all at once in a moment, when obviously the exact truth would not do at all.

"He is a liar, O truly tremendous one!" said one of the drivers. "Several of our people were struck by lightning in the cave, when we invited these creatures to come below; and they are as dead as stones. Also he has not explained this!" He held out the sword which Thorin had worn, the sword which came from the Trolls' lair.

The Great Goblin gave a truly awful howl of rage when he

looked at it, and all his soldiers gnashed their teeth, clashed their shields, and stamped. They knew the sword at once. It had killed hundreds of goblins in its time, when the fair elves of Gondolin hunted them in the hills or did battle before their walls. They had called it Orcrist, Goblin-cleaver, but the goblins called it simply Biter. They hated it and hated worse anyone that carried it.

"Murderers and elf-friends!" the Great Goblin shouted. "Slash them! Beat them! Bite them! Gnash them! Take them away to dark holes full of snakes, and never let them see the light again!" He was in such a rage that he jumped off his seat and himself rushed at Thorin with his mouth open.

Just at that moment, all the lights in the cavern went out, and the great fire went off poof! into a tower of blue glowing smoke, right up to the roof, that scattered piercing white sparks all among the goblins.

The yells and yammering, croaking, jibbering and jabbering; howls, growls and curses; shrieking and skriking, that followed were beyond description. Several hundred wild cats and wolves being roasted slowly alive together would not have compared with it. The sparks were burning holes in the goblins, and the smoke that now fell from the roof made the air too thick for even their eyes to see through. Soon they were falling over one another and rolling in heaps on the floor, biting and kicking and fighting as if they had all gone mad.

Suddenly, a sword flashed in its own light. Bilbo saw it go right through the Great Goblin as he stood dumbfounded in the middle of his rage. He fell dead, and the goblin soldiers fled before the sword shrieking into the darkness.

The sword went back into its sheath. "Follow me quick!" said a voice fierce and quiet; and before Bilbo understood what had happened, he was trotting along again as fast as he could trot, at the end of the line, down more dark passages with the yells of the goblin-hall growing fainter behind him. A pale light was leading them on.

"Quicker, quicker!" said the voice. "The torches will soon be relit."

"Half a minute!" said Dori, who was at the back next to Bilbo, and a decent fellow. He made the hobbit scramble on his shoulders as best he could with his tied hands, and then off they all went at a run, with a clink-clink of chains, and many a stumble, since they had no hands to steady themselves with. Not for a long while did they stop, and by that time they must have been right down in the very mountain's heart.

Then Gandalf lit up his wand. Of course, it was Gandalf; but just then they were too busy to ask how he got there. He took out his sword again, and again it flashed in the dark by itself. It burned with a rage that made it gleam if goblins were about; now it was bright as blue flame for delight in the killing of the great lord of the cave. It made no trouble whatever of cutting through the goblin-chains and setting all the prisoners free as quickly as possible. This sword's name was Glamdring the Foe-hammer, if you remember. The goblins just called it Beater, and hated it worse than Biter if possible. Orcrist, too, had been saved; for Gandalf had brought it along as well, snatching it from one of the terrified guards. Gandalf thought of most things; and though he could not do everything, he could do a great deal for friends in a tight corner.

"Are we all here?" said he, handing his sword back to Thorin with a bow. "Let me see: one – that's Thorin; two, three, four, five, six, seven, eight, nine, ten, eleven; where are Fili and Kili? Here they are! twelve, thirteen – and here's Mr. Baggins: fourteen! Well, well! it might be worse, and then again it might be a good deal better. No ponies, and no food, and no knowing quite where we are, and hordes of angry goblins just behind! On we go!"

On they went. Gandalf was quite right: they began to hear goblin noises and horrible cries far behind in the passages they had come through. That sent them on faster than ever, and as poor Bilbo could not possibly go half as fast – for dwarves can roll along at a tremendous pace, I can tell you, when they have to – they took it in turn to carry him on their backs.

Still, goblins go faster than dwarves, and these goblins knew the way better (they had made the paths themselves) and were madly angry; so that do what they could, the dwarves heard the cries and howls getting closer and closer. Soon they could hear even the flap of the goblin feet, many, many feet which seemed only just around the last corner. The blink of red torches could be seen behind them in the tunnel they were following; and they were getting deadly tired.

"Why, O why did I ever leave my hobbit-hole!" said poor Mr. Baggins, bumping up and down on Bombur's back.

"Why, O why did I ever bring a wretched little hobbit on a treasure hunt!" said poor Bombur, who was fat, and staggered along with the sweat dripping down his nose in his heat and terror.

At this point, Gandalf fell behind, and Thorin with him. They turned a sharp corner. "About turn!" he shouted. "Draw your sword, Thorin!"

There was nothing else to be done; and the goblins did not like it. They came scurrying around the corner in full cry, and found Goblin-cleaver, and Foe-hammer shining cold and bright right in their astonished eyes. The ones in front dropped their torches and gave one yell before they were killed. The ones behind yelled still more and leaped back, knocking over those that were running after them. "Biter and Beater!" they shrieked; and soon they were all in confusion, and most of them were hustling back the way they had come.

It was quite a long while before any of them dared to turn that corner. By that time, the dwarves had gone on again, a long, long, way on into the dark tunnels of the goblins' realm. When the goblins discovered that, they put out their torches, and they slipped on soft shoes, and they chose out their very quickest runners with the sharpest ears and eyes. These ran forward, as swift as weasels in the dark, and with hardly any more noise than bats.

That is why neither Bilbo, nor the dwarves, nor even

Gandalf heard them coming. Nor did they see them. But they were seen by the goblins that ran silently up behind, for Gandalf was letting his wand give out a faint light to help the dwarves as they went along.

Quite suddenly, Dori, now at the back again carrying Bilbo, was grabbed from behind in the dark. He shouted and fell; and the hobbit rolled off his shoulders into the blackness, bumped his head on hard rock, and remembered nothing more.

TRANSFORMATION SCENE

from
VICE VERSA
by
F. ANSTEY

Vice Versa *is a story based on a brilliant comic idea. A rather bad-natured father, by a sort of magical accident, gets himself turned into the perfect image of his own son, while remaining inwardly just as he was: and the boy makes use of the same magic to turn himself into the absolute image of his father, while remaining otherwise wholly a boy. The wicked joy of this idea is worked out fully in the chapters that follow. (I have to say – though I shall say no more – that Mr. Bultitude does end up at Grimstone's Academy, and Dick does take his father's place in an office in the City. With remarkable results!) As this passage opens, the boy Dick is wretchedly waiting for the cab to take him on the first lap of his journey back to school. He has brought into the room a curious stone given him by an uncle of whom his father disapproves. Paul, the father, has confiscated it.*

F. Anstey lived from 1856 to 1924. He wrote another story of comical magic called The Green Bottle.

Paul Bultitude put on his glasses to examine the stone more carefully, for it was some time since he had last seen or thought about it. Then he looked up and said once more, "What use would a thing like this be to you?"

Dick would have considered it a very valuable prize indeed; he could have exhibited it to admiring friends – during lessons, of course, when it would prove a most agreeable distraction; he could have played with and fingered it incessantly, invented astonishing legends of its powers and virtues; and, at last, when he had grown tired of it, have bartered it for any more desirable article that might take his fancy. All these advantages were present to his mind in a vague shifting form, but he could not find either courage or words to explain them.

Consequently, he only said awkwardly, "Oh, I don't know, I should like it."

"Well, anyway," said Paul, "you certainly won't have it. It's worth keeping, whatever it is, as the only thing your uncle Marmaduke was ever known to give to anybody."

Marmaduke Paradine, his brother-in-law, was not a connection of whom he had much reason to feel particularly proud. One of those persons endowed with what are known as "insinuating manners and address," he had, after some futile attempts to enter the army, been sent out to Bombay as agent for a Manchester firm, and in that capacity had contrived to be mixed up in some more than shady transactions with rival exporters and native dealers up the country, which led to unceremonious dismissal by his employers.

He had brought the stone home from India as a propitiatory token of remembrance, more portable and less expensive than the lacquered cabinets, brasses, stuffs, and carved work which are expected from friends at such a distance, and he had been received with pardon and started once more, until certain other proceedings of his, shadier still, had obliged Paul to forbid him entry at Westbourne Terrace.

Since then, little had been heard of him, and the reports which reached Mr. Bultitude of his disreputable relative's connection with the promotion of a series of companies of the kind affected by the widow and curate, and exposed in money articles and law courts, gave him no desire to renew his acquaintance.

"Isn't it a talisman, though?" said Dick, rather unfortunately for any hopes he might have of persuading his father to entrust him with the coveted treasure.

"I'm sure I can't tell you," yawned Paul, "how do you mean?"

"I don't know, only Uncle Duke once said something about it. Barbara heard him tell mama. I say, perhaps it's like the one in Scott, and cures people of things, though I don't think it's that sort of talisman either, because I tried it once on my chilblains, and it wasn't a bit of good. If you would only let me have it, perhaps I might find out, you know."

"You might," said his father drily, apparently not much influenced by this inducement, "but you won't have the chance. If it has a secret, I will find it out for myself" (he little knew how literally he was to be taken at his word), "and, by the way, there's your cab – at last."

There was a sound of wheels outside, and, as Dick heard them, he grew desperate in his extremity; a wish he had long since secretly cherished unspoken, without ever hoping for courage to give it words, rose to his lips now; he got up and moved timidly toward his father.

"Father," he said, "there's something I want to say to you so much before I go. Do let me ask you now."

"Well, what is it?" said Paul. "Make haste, you haven't much time."

"It's this. I want you to – to let me leave Grimstone's at the end of the term."

Paul stared at him, angry and incredulous, "Let you leave Dr. Grimstone's (oblige me by giving him his full title when you speak of him)," he said slowly. "Why, what do you mean? It's an excellent school – never saw a better expressed prospectus in my life. And my old friend Bangle, Sir Benjamin Bangle, who's a member of the School Board, and ought to know something about schools, strongly recommended it – would have sent his own son there, if he hadn't entered him for Eton. And when I pay for most of the extras for you, too. Dancing, by Gad, and meat for breakfast. I'm sure I don't know what you would have."

"I'd like to go to Marlborough, or Harrow, or somewhere," whimpered Dick. "Jolland's going to Harrow at Easter. (Jolland's one of the fellows at Grimstone's – Dr.

Grimstone's, I mean.) And what does old Bangle know about it? He hasn't got to go there himself! And – and Grimstone's jolly enough to fellows he likes, but he doesn't like *me* – he's always sitting on me for something – and I hate some of the fellows there, and altogether it's beastly. Do let me leave! If you don't want me to go to a public school, I – I could stop at home and have a private tutor – like Joe Twitterley!"

"It's all ridiculous nonsense, I tell you," said Paul angrily, "ridiculous nonsense! And, once for all, I'll put a stop to it. I don't approve of public schools for boys like you, and, what's more, I can't afford it. As for private tutors, that's absurd! So you will just make up your mind to stay at Crichton House as long as I think proper to keep you there, and there's an end of that!"

At this final blow to all his hopes, Dick began to sob in a subdued hopeless kind of way, which was more than his father could bear. To do Paul justice, he had not meant to be quite so harsh when the boy was about to set out for school, and, a little ashamed of his irritation, he sought to justify his decision.

He chose to do this by delivering a short homily on the advantages of school, by which he might lead Dick to look on the matter in the calm light of reason and common sense, and commonplaces on the subject began to rise to the surface of his mind, from the rather muddy depths to which they had long since sunk.

He began to give Dick the benefit of all this stagnant wisdom, with a feeling of surprise as he went on, at his own powerful and original way of putting things.

"Now, you know, it's no use to cry like that," he began. "It's – ah – the usual thing for boys at school, I'm quite aware, to go about fancying they're very ill-used, and miserable, and all the rest of it, just as if people in my position had their sons educated out of spite! It's one of those petty troubles all boys have to go through. And you mark my words, my boy, when they go out into the world and have real trials to put up with, and grow middle-aged men, like me, why, they see what fools they've been, Dick; they see what fools they've been. All the – hum – the innocent games and delights of boyhood, and that sort of thing, you know – come back to them – and then they look back to those hours passed at school as the happiest, aye, the very happiest time of their life!"

"Well," said Dick, "then I hope it won't be the happiest time in mine, that's all! And you may have been happy at the school you went to, perhaps, but I don't believe you would very much care about being a boy again like me, and going back to Grimstone's, you know you wouldn't!"

This put Paul on his mettle; he had warmed well to his subject and could not let this open challenge pass unnoticed – it gave him such an opening for a cheap and easy effect.

He still had the stone in his hand as he sank back into his chair, smiling with a tolerant superiority.

"Perhaps you will believe me," he said, impressively, "when, I tell you, old as I am and much as you envy me, I only wish, at this very moment, I could be a boy again, like you. Going back to school wouldn't make me unhappy, I can tell you."

It is so fatally easy to say more than we mean in the desire to make as strong an impression as possible. Well for most of us that – more fortunate than Mr. Bultitude – we can generally do so without fear of being taken too strictly at our word.

As he spoke these unlucky words, he felt a slight shiver, followed by a curious shrinking sensation all over him. It was odd, too, but the armchair in which he sat seemed to have grown so much bigger all at once. He felt a passing surprise, but concluded it must be fancy and went on as comfortably as before.

"I should like it, my boy, but what's the good of wishing? I only mention it to prove that I was not speaking at random. I'm an old man and you're a young boy, and, that being so, why, of course – What the dooce are you giggling about?"

For Dick, after some seconds of half-frightened open-mouthed staring had suddenly burst into a violent fit of almost hysterical giggling, which he seemed trying vainly to suppress.

This naturally annoyed Mr. Bultitude, and he went on with immense dignity, "I – ah – I'm not aware that I've been saying anything particularly ridiculous. You seem to be amused?"

"Don't!" gasped Dick. "It, it isn't anything you're saying – it's, it's – oh, can't you feel any difference?"

"The sooner you go back to school, the better!" said Paul

angrily. "I wash my hands of you. When I do take the trouble to give you any advice, it's received with ridicule. You always were an ill-mannered little cub. I've had quite enough of this. Leave the room, sir!"

The wheels must have belonged to some other cab, for none had stopped at the pavement as yet; but Mr. Bultitude was justly indignant and could stand the interview no longer. Dick, however, made no attempt to move; he remained there, choking and shaking with laughter, while his father sat stiffly on his chair, trying to ignore his son's unmannerly conduct, but only partially succeeding.

No one can calmly endure watching other people laughing at him like idiots, while he is left perfectly incapable of guessing what he has said or done to amuse them. Even when this is known, it requires a peculiarly keen sense of humor to see the point of a joke against oneself.

At last, his patience gave out, and he said coldly, "Now, perhaps, if you are quite yourself again, you will be good enough to let me know what the joke is?"

Dick, looking flushed and half-ashamed, tried again and again to speak, but each time the attempt was too much for him. After a time, he did succeed, but his voice was hoarse and shaken with laughter as he spoke. "Haven't you found it out yet? Go and look at yourself in the glass – it will make you roar!"

There was the usual narrow sheet of plate glass at the back of the sideboard, and to this Mr. Bultitude walked, almost under protest, and with a cold dignity. It occurred to him that he might have a smudge on his face or something wrong with his collar and tie – something to account to some extent for his son's frivolous and insulting behavior. No suspicion of the terrible truth crossed his mind as yet.

Meanwhile, Dick was looking on eagerly with a chuckle of anticipation, as one who watches the dawning appreciation of an excellent joke.

But no sooner had Paul met the reflection in the glass than he started back in incredulous horror – then returned and stared again and again.

Surely, surely, this could not be he!

He had expected to see his own familiar portly bow-windowed presence there – but somehow, look as he would, the mirror insisted upon reflecting the figure of his son Dick. Could he possibly have become invisible and have lost the power of casting a reflection – or how was it that Dick, and only Dick, was to be seen there?

How was it, too, when he looked around, there was the boy still sitting there? It could not be Dick, evidently, that he saw in the glass. Besides, the reflection opposite him moved when he moved, returned when he returned, copied his every gesture!

He turned around upon his son with angry and yet hopeful suspicion. "You, you've been playing some of your infernal tricks with this mirror, sir," he cried fiercely. "What have you done to it?"

"Done! how could I do anything to it? As if you didn't know that!"

"Then," stammered Paul, determined to know the worst, "then do you, do you mean to tell me you can see any – alteration in me? Tell me the truth now!"

"I should just think I could!" said Dick emphatically. "It's very strange, but just look here," and he came up to the sideboard and placed himself by the side of his horrified father. "Why," he said, with another giggle, "we're – he-he – as like as two peas!"

They were indeed; the glass reflected now two small boys, each with chubby cheeks and auburn hair, both dressed, too, exactly alike, in Eton jackets and broad white collars; the only difference to be seen between them was that, while one face wore an expression of intense glee and satisfaction, the other – the one which Mr. Bultitude was beginning to fear must belong to him – was lengthened and drawn with dismay and bewilderment.

"Dick," said Paul faintly, "what is all this? Who has been taking these liberties with me?"

"I'm sure I don't know," protested Dick. "It wasn't me. I believe you did it all yourself."

"Did it all myself!" repeated Paul indignantly. "Is it likely I should? It's some trickery, I tell you, some villainous plot. The worst of it is," he added plaintively, "I don't understand who I'm supposed to be now. Dick, who am I?"

"You can't be me," said Dick, "because here I am, you know. And you're not yourself, that's very plain. You must be *somebody*, I suppose," he added dubiously.

"Of course, I am. What do you mean?" said Paul angrily.

"Never mind who I am. I feel just the same as I always did. Tell me when you first began to notice any change. Could you see it coming on at all, eh?"

"It was all at once, just as you were talking about school and all that. You said you only wished – Why of course; look here, it must be the stone that did it!"

"Stone! what stone?" said Paul. "I don't know what you're talking about."

"Yes, you do – the Garudâ Stone! You've got it in your hand still. Don't you see? It's a real talisman, after all! How jolly!"

"I didn't do anything to set it off; and besides, oh, it's perfectly absurd! How can there be such things as talismans nowadays, eh? Tell me that."

"Well, something's happened to you, hasn't it? And it must have been done somehow," argued Dick.

"I was holding the confounded thing, certainly," said Paul, "here it is. But what could I have said to start it? What has it done this to me for?"

"I know!" cried Dick. "Don't you remember? You said you wished you were a boy again, like me. So you are, you see, exactly like me! What a lark it is, isn't it? But, I say, you can't go up to business like that, you know, can you? I tell you what, you'd better come to Grimstone's with me now, and see how you like it. I shouldn't mind so much if you came, too. Grimstone's face would be splendid when he saw two of us. Do come!"

"That's ridiculous nonsense you're talking," said Paul,

"and you know it. What should I do at school at my age? I tell you I'm the same as ever inside, though I may have shrunk into a little rascally boy to look at. And it's simply an abominable nuisance, Dick, that's what it is! Why on earth couldn't you let the stone alone? Just see what mischief you've done by meddling now – put me to all this inconvenience!"

"You shouldn't have wished," said Dick.

"Wished!" echoed Mr. Bultitude. "Why, to be sure," he said, with a gleam of returning hopefulness, "of course – I never thought of that. The thing's a wishing stone; it must be! You have to hold it, I suppose, and then say what you wish aloud, and there you are. If that's the case, I can soon put it all right by simply wishing myself back again. I – I shall have a good laugh at all this by and by – I know I shall!"

He took the stone and got into a corner by himself where he began repeating the words, "I wish I was back again," "I wish I was the man I was five minutes ago," "I wish all this had not happened," and so on, until he was very exhausted and red in the face. He tried with the stone held in his left hand, as well as his right, sitting and standing, under all the various conditions he could think of, but absolutely nothing came of it; he was just as exasperatingly boyish and youthful as ever at the end of it.

"I don't like this," he said at last, giving it up with a rather crestfallen air. "It seems to me that this diabolical invention has got out of order somehow; I can't make it work any more!"

"Perhaps," suggested Dick, who had shown throughout the most unsympathetic cheerfulness, "perhaps it's one of those talismans that only gives you one wish, and you've had it, you know?"

"Then it's all over!" groaned Paul. "What the dooce am I to do? What shall I do? Suggest something, for Heaven's sake; don't stand cackling there in that unfeeling manner. Can't you see what a terrible mess I've got into? Suppose – only suppose your sister or one of the servants were to come in, and see me like this!"

This suggestion simply enchanted Dick. "Let's have 'em all up," he laughed; "it would be such fun! How they will laugh when we tell them!" And he rushed to the bell.

"Touch that bell if you dare!" screamed Paul. "I won't be seen in this condition by anybody! What on earth could have induced that scoundrelly uncle of yours to bring such a horrible thing as this over I can't imagine! I never heard of such a situation as this in my life. I can't stay like this, you know – it's not to be thought of! I – I wonder whether it would be any use to send over to Dr. Bustard and ask him to step in; he might give me something to bring me 'round. But then the whole neighborhood would hear about it! If I don't see my way out of this soon, I shall go raving mad!"

And he paced restlessly up and down the room with his brain on fire.

All at once, as he became able to think, more coherently, there occurred to him a chance, slender and desperate enough, but still a chance, of escaping even yet the consequences of his folly.

He was forced to conclude that, however improbable and fantastic it might appear in this rationalistic age, there must be some hidden power in this Garudâ Stone which had put him in his present, very unpleasant position. It was plain, too, that the virtues of the talisman refused to exert themselves any more at his bidding.

But it did not follow that in another's hands the spell would remain as powerless. At all events, it was an experiment well worth the trial, and he lost no time in explaining the notion to Dick, who, by the sparkle in his eyes and suppressed excitement in his manner, seemed to think there might be something in it.

"I may as well try," he said, "give it to me."

"Take it, my dear boy," said Paul, with a paternal air that sorely tried Dick's recovered gravity, it contrasted so absurdly with his altered appearance. "Take it, and wish your poor old father himself again!"

Dick took it and held it thoughtfully for some moments, while Paul waited in nervous impatience. "Isn't it any use?" he said dolefully at last, as nothing happened.

"I don't know," said Dick calmly. "I haven't wished yet."

"Then do so at once," said Paul fussily, "do so at once. There's no time to waste, every moment is of importance – your cab will be here directly. Although, although I'm altered in this ridiculous way, I hope I still retain my authority as a father, and as a father, by Gad, I expect you to obey me, sir!"

"Oh, all right," said Dick indifferently, "you may keep the authority if you like."

"Then do what I tell you. Can't you see how urgent it is that a scandal like this shouldn't get about? I should be the laughing-stock of the city. Not a soul must ever guess that such a thing has happened. You must see that yourself."

"Yes," said Dick, who all this time was sitting on a corner of the table, swinging his legs, "I see that. It will be all right. I'm going to wish in a minute, and no one will guess there has been anything the matter."

"That's a good boy!" said Paul, much relieved, "I know your heart is in the right place – only do make haste."

"I suppose," Dick asked, "when you are yourself again, things would go on just as usual?"

"I – I hope so."

"I mean you will go on sitting here, and I shall go off to Grimstone's?"

"Of course, of course," said Paul; "don't ask so many questions. I'm sure you quite understand what has to be done, so get on. We might be found like this any minute."

"That settles it," said Dick, "any fellow would do it after that."

"Yes, yes, but you're so slow about it!"

"Don't be in a hurry," said Dick, "you mayn't like it after all when I've done it."

"Done what?" asked Mr. Bultitude sharply, struck by something sinister and peculiar in the boy's manner.

"Well, I don't mind telling you," said Dick, "it's fairer.

You see, you wished to be a boy just like me, didn't you?"

"I didn't mean it," protested Paul.

"Ah, you couldn't expect a stone to know that; at any rate, it made you into a boy like me directly. Now, if I wish myself a man just like you were ten minutes ago, before you took the stone, that will put things all right again, won't it?"

"Is the boy mad?" cried Paul, horrified at this proposal. "Why, why, that would be worse than ever!"

"I don't see that," objected Dick, stubbornly. "No one would know anything about it then."

"But, you little blockhead, can't I make you understand? It wouldn't do at all. We should both of us be wrong then – each with the other's personal appearance."

"Well," said Dick blandly, "I shouldn't mind that."

"But I should – I mind very much. I object strongly to such a – such a preposterous arrangement. And what's more, I won't have it. Do you hear, I forbid you to think of any such thing. Give me back that stone. I can't trust you with it after this."

"I can't help it," said Dick doggedly. "You've had your wish, and I don't see why I shouldn't have mine. I mean to have it, too."

"Why, you unnatural little rascal!" cried the justly-enraged father, "do you mean to defy me? I tell you I will have that stone! Give it up this instant!" and he made a movement toward his son, as if he meant to recover the talisman by main force.

But Dick was too quick for him. Slipping off the table with

great agility, he planted himself firmly on the hearth-rug, with the hand that held the stone clenched behind his back, and the other raised in self-defense.

"I'd much rather you wouldn't make me hit you, you know," he said, "because, in spite of what's happened, you're still my father, I suppose. But if you interfere with me before I've done with this stone, I'm afraid I shall have to punch your head."

Mr. Bultitude retreated a few steps apprehensively, feeling himself no match for his son, except in size and general appearance; and for some moments of really frightful intensity, they stood panting on the hearth-rug, each cautiously watching the other, on his guard against stratagem and surprise.

It was once of those painful domestic scenes which are fortunately rare between father and son.

Overhead, the latest rollicking French polka was being rattled out, with a savage irony of which pianos, even by the best makers, can at times be capable.

Suddenly, Dick drew himself up. "Stand out of my way!" he cried excitedly, "I am going to do it. I wish I was a man like you were just now!"

And as he spoke, Mr. Bultitude had the bitterness of seeing his unscrupulous son swell out like the frog in the fable, till he stood there before him the exact duplicate of what Paul had so lately been!

The transformed Dick began to skip and dance around the room in high glee, with as much agility as his increased bulk would allow. "It's all right, you see," he said. "The old stone's as good as ever. You can't say anyone would ever know, to look at us."

And then he threw himself panting into a chair, and began to laugh excitedly at the success of his unprincipled maneuvers.

As for Paul, he was perfectly furious at having been so outwitted and overreached. It was a long time before he could command his voice sufficiently to say, savagely: "Well, you've had your way, and a pretty mess you've made of it. We're both of us in false positions now. I hope you're satisfied, I'm sure. Do you think you'll care about going back to Crichton House in that state?"

"No," said Dick, very decidedly: "I'm quite sure I shouldn't."

"Well, I can't help it. You've brought it on yourself; and, provided the Doctor sees no objection to take you back as you are and receive you as one of his pupils, I shall most certainly send you there."

Paul did not really mean this, he only meant to frighten him; for he still really trusted that, by letting Boaler into the secret, the charm might be set in motion once more, and the difficulty comfortably overcome. But his threat had a most unfortunate effect upon Dick; it hardened him to take a course he might otherwise have shrunk from.

"Oh," he said, "you're going to do that? But doesn't it strike you that things are rather altered with us now?"

"They are, to a certain extent, of course," said Paul,

"through my folly and your wicked cunning; but a word or two of explanation from me –"

"You'll find it will take more explanation than you think," said Dick; "but, of course, you can try, if you think it worth while – when you get to Grimstone's."

"When I, – I don't understand. When I, – what did you say?" gasped Paul.

"Why, you see," exclaimed Dick, "it would never have done for us both to go back; the chaps would have humbugged us so, and as I hate the place and you seem so fond of being a boy and going back to school and that, I thought perhaps it would be best for you to go and see how you liked it!"

"I never will! I'll not stir from this room! I dare you to try to move me!" cried Paul. And just then there was the sound of wheels outside once more. They stopped before the house, the bell rang sharply – the long-expected cab had come at last.

"You've no time to lose," said Dick, "get your coat on."

Mr. Bultitude tried to treat the affair as a joke. He laughed a ghastly little laugh.

"Ha! ha! you've fairly caught your poor father this time; you've proved him in the wrong. I admit I said more than I exactly meant. But that's enough. Don't drive a good joke too far; shake hands, and let us see if we can't find a way out of this!"

But Dick only warmed his coat tails at the fire as he said, with a very ungenerous reminiscence of his father's manner:

"You are going back to an excellent establishment, where you will enjoy all the comforts of home – I can specially recommend the stickjaw; look out for it on Tuesdays and Fridays. You will once more take part in the games and lessons of happy boyhood. (Did you ever play "chevy" when you were a boy before? You'll enjoy chevy.) And you will find your companions easy enough to get on with, if you don't go giving yourself airs; they won't stand airs. Now good-bye, my boy, and bless you!"

Paul stood staring stupidly at this outrageous assumption; he could scarcely believe yet that it was meant in cruel earnest. Before he could answer, the door opened, and Boaler appeared.

"Had a deal of trouble to find a keb, sir, on a night like this," he said to the false Dick, "but the luggage is all on top, and the man says there's plenty of time still."

"Good-bye, then, my boy," said Dick, with well-assumed tenderness, but a rather dangerous light in his eye. "My compliments to the Doctor, remember."

Paul turned indignantly from him to the butler; he, at least, would stand by him. Boaler would not see a master who had always been fair, if not indulgent, to him driven from his home in this cold-blooded manner!

He made two or three attempts to speak, for his brain so whirled with scathing, burning things to say. He would expose the fraud then and there, and defy the impudent usurper; he would warn every one against this spurious pinchbeck imitation of himself. The whole household should be summoned and called upon to judge between the two!

No doubt, if he had had enough self-command to do all this effectually, while Dick had as yet not had the time thoroughly to adapt himself to his altered circumstances, he might have turned the situation at the outset and thus saved himself some very painful experiences.

But it is very often precisely those words which are the most vitally important to be said that refuse to pass our lips in a sudden emergency. We feel all the necessity of saying something at once, but the necessary words unaccountably desert us at the critical moment.

Mr. Bultitude felt himself in this unfortunate position. He made more wild efforts to explain, but the sense of his danger only petrified his mind instead of stimulating it. Then he was spared further conflict. A dark mist rose before his eyes; the walls of the room receded into infinite space; and, with a loud singing in his ears, he fell and seemed to himself to be sinking down, down, through the earth to the very crust of the antipodes. Then the blackness closed over him – and he knew no more.

THROUGH THE DOOR

from
TOM'S MIDNIGHT GARDEN
by
PHILIPPA PEARCE

Tom's Midnight Garden *is a story concerned, strangely and wonderfully, with the mysteries of Time. Tom is spending a vacation, not very happily, with an uncle and aunt. He discovers that the grandfather clock in the hall strikes an hour that doesn't exist, the hour of thirteen, and that when this happens and he steps into the walled garden of the house, he is stepping out of present time. Night after night, he does this, and always it is a different moment of past time in the garden, and always he is*

invisible, except to one little girl...

Philippa Pearce, born in 1920, has also written The Minnow on the Say, *a completely unusual story of a treasure hunt, and, among other books,* A Dog Too Small *and two marvelous picture books called* Mrs. Cockle's Cat *and* Lion at School.

E very night now, Tom slipped downstairs to the garden. At first, he used to be afraid that it might not be there. Once, with his hand already upon the garden door to open it, he had turned back, sick with grief at the very thought of absence. He had not dared, then, to look; but, later the same night, he had forced himself to go again and open that door: there the garden was. It had not failed him.

He saw the garden at many times of its day, and at different seasons – its favorite season was summer, with perfect weather. In earliest summer, hyacinths were still out in the crescent beds on the lawn, and wallflowers in the round ones. Then the hyacinths bowed and died; and the wallflowers were uprooted, and stocks and asters bloomed in their stead. There was a clipped box bush by the greenhouse, with a cavity like a great mouth cut into the side of it: this was stacked full of pots of geraniums in flower. Along the sundial path, heavy red poppies came out, and roses; and, in summer dusk, the evening primroses glimmered like little moons. In the latest summer, the pears on the wall were muffled in muslin bags for safe ripening.

Tom was not a gardener, however; his first interest in a garden was tree-climbing. He always remembered his first tree in this garden – one of the yews around the lawn. He had never climbed a yew before and was inclined to think ever afterward that yews were best.

The first branches grew conveniently low, and the main trunk had bosses and crevices. With the toes of his left foot fitted into one of these last, Tom curved his hands around the branch over his head. Then he gave a push, a spring, and a strong haul on the arms: his legs and feet were dangling free, and the branch was under his chest, and then under his middle. He drew himself still farther forward, at the same time twisting himself expertly: now he was sitting on the bough, a man's height above ground.

The rest of the ascent was easy, but interesting: sometimes among the spreading, outermost branches; sometimes working close to the main trunk. Tom loved the dry feel of the bark on the main trunk. In places, the bark had peeled away and then a deep pink showed beneath, as though the tree were skin and flesh beneath its brown.

Up he went – up and up, and burst at last from the dim interior into an openness of blue and fiery gold. The sun was the gold, in a blue sky. All around him was a spreading, tufted surface of evergreen. He was on a level with all the yew-tree tops around the lawn; nearly on a level with the top of the tall south wall.

Tom was on a level, too, with the upper windows of the house, just across the lawn from him. His attention was caught by a movement inside one of the rooms: it came, he saw, from the same maid he had once seen in the hall. She was dusting a bedroom, and came now to the window to raise the sash and shake her duster outside. She looked casually across to the yew-trees as she did so, and Tom tried waving to her. It was like waving to the It in blindman's-buff.

The maid went back into the depths of the room, to her dusting. She left the window open behind her, and Tom could now see more. There was someone else in the room besides the maid – someone who stood against the far wall, facing the window. The maid evidently spoke to her companion occasionally as she worked, for Tom could hear the faint coming and going of voices. He could not see the other figure at all clearly, except that it was motionless, and there was the whiteness and shape of a face that was always turned in his direction. That steadfastness of direction embarrassed Tom. Gradually he began to draw his head downward, and then suddenly ducked it below tree-level altogether.

Tom saw more people later, in the garden itself. He stalked them warily, and yet – remembering his invisibility to the housemaid – with a certain confidence, too.

He was pretty sure that the garden was used more often than he knew. He often had the feeling of people having just gone – and an uncomfortable feeling, out of which he tried to reason himself, again and again, of someone who had *not* gone: someone who, unobserved, observed him. It was a relief really to see people, even when they ignored his presence: the maid, the gardener, and a severe-looking woman in a long dress of rustling purple silk, face to face with whom Tom once came unexpectedly, on a corner. She cut him dead.

Visibility... invisibility... If he were invisible to the people of the garden, he was not completely so at least to some of the other creatures. How truly they saw him he could not say; but birds cocked their heads at him and flew away when he approached.

And had he any bodily weight in this garden, or had he not? At first, Tom thought not. When he climbed the yew-tree, he had been startled to feel that no bough swung beneath him, and not a twig broke. Later – and this was a great disappointment to him – he found that he could not, by the ordinary grasping and pushing of his hand, open any of the doors in the garden, to go through them. He could not push open the door of the greenhouse or of the little heating-house behind it, or the door in the south wall by the sundial.

The doors shut against Tom were a check upon his curiosity, until he saw a simple way out: he would get through the doorways that interested him by following at the heels of the gardener. He regularly visited the greenhouse, the heating-house, and used the south wall door.

Tom concentrated upon getting through the south wall door. That entry promised to be the easiest, because the gardener went through so often, with his tools. There must be a tool-shed somewhere through there.

The gardener usually went through so quickly and shut the door so smartly behind him, that there was not time for anyone else to slip through as well. However, he would be slower with a wheelbarrow, Tom judged; and he waited patiently for that opportunity. Yet even then, the man somehow only made a long arm to open the door ahead of the wheelbarrow, wheeled it very swiftly through, caught the door-edge with the toe of his boot as he passed, and slammed the door in Tom's face.

Tom glared at the door that once more was his barrier. Once more, without hope, he raised his hand to the latch and pressed it. As usual, he could not move it: his fingers seemed to have no substance. Then, in anger, he pressed with all imaginable might: he knitted his brows and brought all his will to bear upon the latch, until he felt that something had to happen. It did: his fingers began to go through the latch, as though the latch, and not his fingers, now, were without substance. His fingers went through the ironwork of the latch altogether, and his hand fell back into place by his side.

Tom stared down at that ever-memorable right hand. He felt it tenderly with his left, to see if it were bruised or broken: it was quite unhurt – quite as before. Then he looked at the latch: it looked as real as any latch he had ever seen anywhere.

Then the idea came to Tom that the door might be no more solid than the latch, if he really tried it.

Deliberately, he set his side against the door, shoulder, hip, and heel, and pressed. At first, nothing gave, either of himself or the door. Yet he continued the pressure, with still greater force and greater determination; and gradually he became aware of a strange sensation, that at first he thought was a numbness all down his side – but no, it was not that.

"I'm going through," Tom gasped, and was seized with alarm and delight.

On the other side of the wall, the gardener had emptied his barrow-load of weeds and was sitting on the handle of his barrow, in front of a potting shed, eating his midday dinner. If he had been able to see Tom at all, he would have seen a most curious sight: a very thin slice of boy, from shoulder to foot, coming through a perfectly solid wooden door. At first, the body came through evenly from top to bottom; then, the upper part seemed to stop, and the bottom part came through in its entirety, legs first. Then one arm came through, then another. Finally, everything was through except the head.

The truth was that Tom was now a little lacking courage. The passing through the door of so much of his body had not been without enormous effort and peculiar, if indescribable, sensations. "I'm just resting a minute," said Tom's head, on the garden side of the door; yet he knew that he was really delaying because he was nervous. His stomach, for instance, had felt most uncomfortable as it passed through the door; what would the experience be like for his head – his eyes, his ears?

On the other hand – and the new idea was even worse than the old – supposing that, like a locomotive-engine losing steam-pressure, he lost his present force of body and will-power in this delay? Then, he would be unable to move either forward or backward. He would be caught here by the neck, perhaps forever. And just supposing someone came along, on the far side of the wall, who by some evil chance *could* see him – supposing a whole company came: they would see an entirely defenseless stern sticking out – an invitation to ridicule and attack.

With a convulsive effort, eyes closed, lips sealed, Tom dragged his head through the door, and stood, dizzy, dazed, but whole, on the far side of it.

When his vision cleared, he saw that he was standing directly in front of the potting shed and the gardener. Tom had never been front to front with the gardener before: he was a large-framed young man, with a weather-reddened face, and eyes the color of the sky itself – they now looked straight through Tom and far away. Into his mouth, he was putting the last fragments of a thick bacon-and-bread sandwich. He finished the sandwich, closed his eyes and spoke aloud: "For all good things, I thank the Lord; and may He keep me from all the works of the Devil that he hurt me not."

He spoke with a country voice, clipping short his t's and widening his vowels, so that Tom had to listen attentively to understand him.

The gardener opened his eyes again, and, reaching behind him, brought out another sandwich. Tom wondered, in some surprise, whether he said grace after every sandwich. Perhaps he never knew how many he was going to eat.

The gardener went on eating, and Tom turned away to look around him. He was in an orchard, that also served for the keeping of hens, the hanging out of washing, and the kindling of a bonfire. Beyond the orchard were meadows and trees, from among which rose the roofs of what must be a village.

While he looked, Tom was also keeping a sharp eye upon the gardener. When the man had really finished his meal, he grasped the handles of his wheelbarrow, to return to his work in the garden. In a moment, Tom was beside him. He had not at all enjoyed the experience of going through a shut door, and he did not now intend to have to repeat it. This time, there was an easy way through: he got nimbly up into the empty barrow and was wheeled back into the garden in comfort.

It was a long time before Tom literally forced his way through a door again. Anyway, he had seen the orchard, and that was enough in that direction; other doors could wait. Meanwhile, he climbed the low wall at the bottom of the garden and explored the woods, beyond. On the third side of the garden, he wormed his way through the hedge again and crossed the meadow. The only surprise there was the boundary: a river, clear, gentle-flowing, shallow, and green with reeds and water plants.

The garden and its surroundings, then, were not, in themselves, outside the natural order of things; nor was Tom alarmed by his own unnatural abilities. Yet, to some things, his mind came back again and again, troubled: the constant good weather, the rapid coming and going of the seasons and the times of day, the feeling of being watched.

One night, all his uneasiness came to a head. He had gone from his bed in the room upstairs and crept down to the hall at about midnight, as usual; he had opened the garden door. He had found for the first time that it was night, too, in the garden. The moon was up, but clouds fled continuously across its face. Although there was this movement in the upper air, down below there was none: a great stillness lay within the garden, and a heavier heat than at any noon. Tom felt it: he unbuttoned his pajama jacket and let it flap open as he walked.

He could smell the storm coming. Before Tom had reached the end of the garden, the moon had disappeared, obscured altogether by cloud. In its place came another light that seemed instantaneously to split the sky from top to bottom, and a few seconds later came the thunder.

Tom turned back to the house. As he reached the porch, the winds broke out into the lower air, with heavy rain and a deathly chilling of the temperature. Demons of the air seemed let loose in that garden; and, with the increasing frequency of the lightning, Tom could watch the foliage of the trees ferociously tossed and torn at by the wind, and, at the corner of the lawn, the tall, tapering fir tree swinging to and fro, its ivy-wreathed arms struggling wildly in the tempest like the arms of a swaddling-child.

To Tom, it seemed that the fir tree swung more widely

each time. "It can't be blown over," thought Tom. "Strong trees are not often blown over."

As if in answer to this, and while the winds still tore, there came the loudest thunder, with a flash of lightning that was not to one side nor even above, but seemed to come down into the garden itself, to the tree. The glare was blinding, and Tom's eyes closed against it, although only for a part of a second. When he opened them again, he saw the tree like one flame, and falling. In the long instant while it fell, there seemed to be a horrified silence of all the winds; and, in that quiet, Tom heard something – a human cry – an 'Oh!' of the terror he himself felt. It came from above him – from the window of one of the upper rooms.

Then the fir tree fell, stretching its length – although Tom did not know this until much later – along the beds of the asparagus in the vegetable garden. It fell in darkness and the resumed rushing of wind and rain.

Tom was shaken by what he had seen and heard. He went back into the house and shut the garden door behind him. Inside, the grandfather clock ticked peacefully; the hall was still. He wondered if perhaps he had only imagined what he had seen outside. He opened the door again and looked out. The summer storm was still raging. The flashes of lightning were distant now: they lit up the ugly gap in the trees around the lawn, where the fir tree had stood.

The tree had fallen, that had been a sight terrible enough; but the cry from above troubled Tom more. On the next night came the greatest shock of all. He opened the garden door as usual and surveyed the garden. At first, he did not understand what was odd in its appearance; then, he realized that its usual appearance was in itself an oddity. In the trees around the lawn, there was no gap: the ivy-grown fir tree still towered above them.

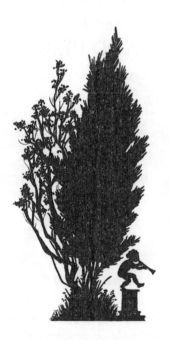

THE EMPEROR'S NEW CLOTHES

by

HANS CHRISTIAN ANDERSEN

retold by

EDWARD BLISHEN

Andersen (who lived from 1805 to 1875) was an astonishing Dane, largely self-educated, whose life was as extraordinary as any of the tales he told. There were over one hundred and fifty of these stories, some of them among the most famous ever written by anyone. They are sometimes called fairy stories, but fairies rarely appear in them: in the best, a completely original imagination is at work. As it is, certainly, in the tale that follows.

T here was once (long ago, of course) an Emperor. Nothing pleased him half as much as buying new clothes and appearing in them. You could keep the army, as far as he was concerned, or the theater: and as for going around his kingdom, he was interested in doing that only when it made it possible for him to show off a new set of clothes. He was never known to wear the same coat for more than two hours running, and much of his life was spent in his great dressing room.

One day, two strangers, who said they were weavers, turned up in the imperial city. They made a tremendous fuss about the cloth they wove. Very fine, very handsome, they said: but magical, too. Well, it was like this: if you had a stupid person, he just would not be able to see any costume made from that cloth. It would be invisible.

The Emperor would have been interested anyway, a new kind of cloth being exactly what he was looking for: but it struck him that this might be a way of discovering who among his ministers and officials was worth his pay, and who was not. Anyone who could see the clothes that would be made for the Emperor by the newcomers could keep his job: but the rest he would get rid of.

So he summoned the two rascals (for that is what they were) and gave them gold, so that they could start their weaving.

And that is what they did. Or to be more truthful, that is what they pretended to do. They set up two looms and sat in front of them, doing all those things you have to do if you want to weave cloth: the difference being that... on the looms, there was nothing at all. Not a single strand of anything. Of course, they asked for (and got) the best silk, the finest gold thread. This they stowed away, to be sold later; and then they sat again in front of the looms and put on an appearance of being enormously busy. Which, enormously, they were not.

After a while, the Emperor was anxious to see how things were going. However, he was a little worried. If you were stupid, you'd not be able to see the cloth at all. Now, of course... *he* was the Emperor, and there was no question of his being stupid: but all the same... Better, perhaps, as a first step, to send someone else along to see how good this cloth was...

Among his ministers, there was one thought of by all as perhaps the most honest and intelligent man in the world. He was obviously the right man for this, and the Emperor lost no time in asking him to visit the weavers. The good old man found the two rascals apparently hard at work. Their fingers were moving up and down, and this way and that, at great speed, but... Nothing was to be seen. "Good gracious!" thought the old minister. "Oh, my goodness!" There was (he rubbed his eyes) nothing there (he put on his glasses) – nothing at all!

The rascals urged him to come closer. "Handsome patterns, eh, sir?" "Aren't these colors *beautiful*!" The old man put on a second pair of glasses. There was still nothing to be seen. Perhaps, he thought, he *was* stupid! But... he did so very much enjoy being a minister! What should he do? Surely it was best to pretend he *could* see the cloth. "Delightful!" he cried. "Never seen anything like it! Marvelous!" And so on. "The Emperor *will* be pleased!"

"Are you sure of that?" asked those rascals, pretending to be anxious. "Will he really like... the leaves, here – and this... row of flowers and – this... *very* dark blue?" "Oh, yes, he will like them – I am sure he will like them!" cried the old minister.

And off he went to report to the Emperor. "Your Majesty," he said. "Indeed, the cloth is *superb!*"

Soon the whole town was talking about this wonderful cloth; and the Emperor decided it was safe for him to go and inspect it himself – together, of course, with some of his most trusted officials, including the old minister. In the weaving room, the rascals were still making the movements a weaver ought to make – up and over and in and out, and in and over and up and out – and their feet busy on the pedals and, on their faces, looks of such satisfaction: but... there was *nothing* there.

"Oh, those patterns, sire!" cried the old minister. "Oh, those *colors!*"

"Heavens!" thought the Emperor. "I can't see a thing! I can't see a pattern of any kind, or any sort of color! Am I stupid? But, of course, that cannot be! I am the Emperor!" So he smiled and nodded and said "Oh, wonderful! Oh, beautiful! We admire it very much!" As for his officials and the courtiers, they stared at the empty looms and the fast-moving fingers of the weavers. "Wonderful! Beautiful!" they cried. "And, oh, Your Majesty... remember the procession that is to take place next Tuesday? How marvelous if you wore for that a set of robes made of this most elegant material!" The Emperor beamed. Everyone beamed. And on the spot, the Emperor invented a brand-new honor for those rascals: they were appointed the very first Grand Masters of the Imperial Loom.

And so (because next Tuesday was not far off) the rascals worked all night, or pretended to do so, among candles burning in their hundreds: and they pretended to take the material off the looms, and they pretended to cut it with their scissors: and finally they pretended to stitch it with needles that had no thread in them (though no one dared to say so): and late on Monday night came the cry: "The Emperor's clothes are ready!"

So the Emperor and his courtiers came to the weaving room, and the rascals displayed the new clothes as if they actually existed. They'd lift up something that wasn't really there and would cry: "Here are the imperial trousers!" And again: "Here is the imperial jacket!" And again: "Here is the imperial cravat!" And (pretending to take great care not to crease it): "*Here* is the imperial cloak! All," they said, "are as light as if they were cobwebs. Wearing them, Your Majesty, you will imagine" (and they lowered their voices) "that you have nothing on at all."

"Ah! Ah, yes!" murmured the imperial officials.

"And so," cried the rascals, "if Your Majesty would take off what he is now wearing, and step in front of the mirror, we will fit him with his new clothes."

And that's what happened. That is to say, the Emperor took off his actual clothes and stood naked in front of the mirror, and the rascals handed him his imaginary trousers, and he believed he was putting them on: and his imaginary shirt, and he believed he was putting *that* on: and so on till they came to his great (imaginary) imperial train, and he believed he was putting that on, too.

"Marvelous! A most beautiful fit! Suits Your Majesty perfectly!" everyone murmured, ministers and courtiers and officials and rascals together, as the Emperor turned this way and that and admired himself in the long mirror. "Wonderful patterns! Superb colors! We've never seen more magnificent imperial robes, ever!"

"It is time, Your Majesty," cried the old minister, "for the procession. If Your Majesty would step under the canopy…"

And the Emperor declared: "I am ready! Wonderful, don't you think – wonderful!" And the bearers of the canopy stepped forward, and the Emperor (clad only, as it happened, in his crown) stepped under it, and his attendants picked up the imperial train, or pretended to: for in fact there was nothing there.

And so the procession set off through the streets. People were watching from the sidewalks and from the windows of buildings, and they all cried: "The Emperor has never looked more splendid! How magnificently he is dressed!

Such *wonderful* new clothes!"

The fact is that no one wanted to admit there was nothing to be seen: because no one wanted to be thought to be stupid.

But then a voice was raised. It was a child's. *"The Emperor has nothing on!"* she cried. "Oh," said her father, "these children! You don't know what they'll say next!" And he shook the child angrily. But the people standing next to them murmured: "This child says the Emperor has nothing on: and now she's mentioned it, *we* think he has nothing on." And the people standing next to them said the same thing: and soon the whole crowd was muttering: "But the fact is, the Emperor has nothing on!" And all that muttering and murmuring at last reached the ears of the Emperor himself: and he thought, "They are right! I have *nothing* on!"

But he was too proud to admit this: so, stark naked under the canopy, he continued processing through the town, and his attendants followed him pretending to lift the train: though they knew perfectly well that, like the rest of the Emperor's new clothes, it wasn't there at all.

WHO'LL TEACH SMITH TO READ?

from
SMITH
by
LEON GARFIELD

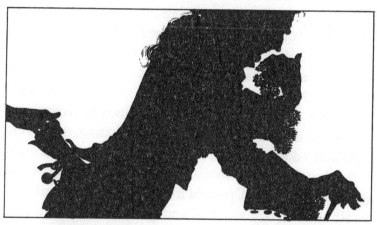

Leon Garfield was born in 1921; but he writes about the 1700s (and especially about London, England, in the 1700s) as if it were then, and there, that he was alive. One of his best stories set in London around 1750 is Smith. Smith *is twelve years old, "a sooty spirit of the violent and ramshackle Town," who makes a desperate living by picking pockets and is fortunately very fast on his feet: "A rat was like a snail beside Smith." One morning, he picks the pocket of an old gentleman: and almost at once sees the old man set upon and murdered and his clothes searched by*

the murderers, who fail to find what they are looking for. That, clearly, is what Smith has stolen, which turns out to be a document. One worth murdering for! But alas, Smith cannot read...

Leon Garfield has written many novels in which he combines a gift for tickling your ribs with a gift for chilling your spine: Black Jack *and* John Diamond *are highly recommended, and a series of shorter, connected stories published as* The Apprentices.

 tremendous idea had lodged in Smith's mind and, like all truly great things, answered its purpose so exactly that one exclaimed, "Why hadn't it been thought of before?" He would *learn* to read!

The morning was dull and windy. The cathedral birds were huddled upon Old Bailey, which stood on the leeward side of the stench from Newgate Jail. Such merchants and clerks and attorneys who walked the whipping streets kept their heads down and their hands to their wigs and hats – as if to hold their aspiring thoughts from flying out to become common property. A general frown and scowl creased their faces: another day was bad enough, without the insolent wind aggravating it!

Smith had spread the document inside his coat and across his chest, where it kept him from the worst of the weather.

"Be still, old fellow," he muttered from time to time as the stiff paper pricked and tickled. "You and me's got business. You and me's going up in the world... just as soon as I gets you to talk!"

He was crossing Ludgate Hill when, suddenly, he fancied he saw the murdered old gentleman, stumping along ahead of him. He stopped, much frightened. Then he looked again and saw that the old gentleman was someone else altogether. But thereafter the murdered man stayed pretty firmly in his thoughts – as if keeping a watch on his document and where Smith was taking it.

Which, in the first place, was to the blackened and gloomy felonage of Newgate Jail. Smith turned in at the lodge, greeted the jailer there, and lit up his battered pipe against the dreadful smells to come.

First, he found out Mr. Jones, the hangman: a short, stout, rough-handed gent who shone with pomatum. He got three shillings out of him on account – together with a surly prophecy that if he, Smith, didn't mind his *P's* and *Q's* he'd become Mr. Jones's customer in a transaction with a yardage of hemp.

"*P's* and *Q's*?" said Smith, earnestly. "Them's letters, ain't they?"

Mr. Jones agreed.

"Then show us a *P*, Mister Jones, and then show us a *Q*, and I'll try to mind 'em!"

For the thought had occurred to Smith that two letters would be a fair start to the day's work of learning to read. Unluckily, Mr. Jones took him for a humorist and aimed a thump that would have been pleasurable if it had struck.

Bleeding scholars! thought Smith, as he scuttled out of the hangman's office. Want to keep everything to themselves!

From Mr. Jones's, it was but a brief, though dark and sullen, way down a ragged stairway, along a passage, a turn to the right, then up two steps, to the Stone Hall, where Smith's present hopes were most likely to be passing the time of what was neither night nor day. The Stone Hall was a long, low, arched room with its own stone sky and its own six lanterns for a sun. When these were lit, it was day, when they were out, it was night – no matter what the outside heavens were declaring.

Smith's present hopes shuffled somewhere among the lost multitude of the Town's garbage and dregs. Grumbling rag-bags and tattered felons, debtors who always looked surprised and, here and there, like a fallen moon, a pale white face of unbroken pride – most likely of a man due to be hanged.

Here was Smith's place of daily business; for he ran errands for the debtors – twopence a mile dry, and fourpence when it rained.

Very educated gentlemen, the debtors. A man needs to be educated to get into debt. Scholars all. The first Smith tried was a tall, fine-looking gentleman who, though still in leg-irons, walked like he owned the jail – as well he might, for his debts could have bought it entire.

He smiled; he was never at a loss for a smile... which was, perhaps, why he was there; when a man can't pay what he owes, a smile is a deal worse than nothing!

"Learn us to read, mister!" said Smith, humbly.

The fine debtor, stopped, looked – and sighed.

"Not in ten thousand years, my boy!" and, before Smith

could ask him why, he told him.

"Be happy that you can't! For what will you get by it? You'll read and fret over disasters that might never touch you. You'll read hurtful letters that might have passed you by. You'll read warrants and summonses where you might have pleaded ignorance. You'll read of bills overdue and creditors' anger – where you might have ignored it all for another month! Don't learn to read, Smith! Oh! I implore you!"

Then the gentleman drifted, smiling, away, with his back straight, his head held high – and his ankles jingling.

Next, Smith applied to a learned felon, a ferret-faced man with small, starry eyes.

"What d'yer want to read for, Smith? No need. And if it weren't for me skill as a reader, I'd not be here today. I was on the run – and saw a new goldsmith's sign. Stopped to read it – and 'ere I am! No, stay ignorant, me boy – and keep out of 'arm's way."

Smith pleaded – but the felon was determined, so Smith left him and would have gone from the Stone Hall had he not seen Mr. Palmer.

This Mr. Palmer was a debtor of a different sort: a gentle, sad man who could not bring himself to believe that the world had been so spiteful as to jail him. (Even though it had been these past five years.) For Mr. Palmer – did the world but know it – nourished a very high opinion of himself, which he was careful to hide for fear of its being damaged.

"Learn us to read, Mister Palmer!"

Mr. Palmer stopped in mid-shuffle.

"Learn us to read, Mister Palmer!"

Mr. Palmer turned on Smith a look of amazement that hid a powerful contempt and dislike – even loathing – for this debtor loathed, hated, and despised every mortal thing that was better off than himself by being free.

"A pleasure to *'learn'* you, Smith," he said. "Here, boy." He bent down and beckoned. Smith approached. "This is how we begin!"

He seized Smith's nose as hard as he could and pulled and twisted and wrenched it till Smith's squeals filled the Stone Hall and his eyes fairly gushed with tears. Then his own voice was raised even louder, in a fearful bellow of pain. He'd forgotten Smith wore no leg-irons and could use his feet to advantage.

In an instant, Smith was fled, leaving Mr. Palmer with an empty finger and thumb, and a pair of shins that were splintered with booting. He lay on the ground and continued to roar, only breaking off to pray that the ungrateful brat who'd crippled him might come to a bad end on Mr. Jones's rope; while Smith, full of anger and humiliation and a burning pain in his nose, left Newgate Jail swearing a solemn oath that, not till he was took, would he ever set foot in that foul place again!

With his hands pressed to his chest and his eyes still streaming with forced tears, he ran toward the nestling of lanes about the great cathedral. Soft-hearted ladies stared as he passed, moved by the sight of the weeping urchin. Then his eyes dried up, his nose recovered – and his grand determination flared anew. He *would* learn to read! For he and the document were going up in the world – though the Devil himself stood against them!

Surely the Town had more scholars than those in Newgate Jail? The streets must be full of them! He'd only to ask. No harm in asking... He crossed the windy street to meet a round-faced old gentleman with an absent-minded air.

"Mister – mister! Learn me to read!"

The gentleman paused – momentarily taking his hand from his hat. In an instant, the wind whipped it off, together with his wig, leaving him as bald as the dome of St. Paul's. Smith, meaning no offence, began to grin. The gentleman raised his stick – and Smith fled for his life!

He asked a lawyer, a clerk, a country schoolmaster – but they'd have none of him. He poked his head through the window of a carriage waiting outside an apothecary's to ask of the elderly lady sat within. But she shrieked and shouted for her footman to frighten him off. At last, he found himself in Holborn Hill, passing by gray, high-shouldered St. Andrew's Church. The Church: Mother of the Town – and all creatures in it!

With renewed hope, he shuffled up to the porch and peered into the richly stained gloom of the church's insides. Blood of glass martyrs fell across the aisle and drenched the altar... and there was a smell of damp stone in the quiet air. A very peaceful, genteel sort of place.

At first, it seemed empty – and Smith had some brief

thoughts concerning the candlesticks.

"What d'you want, my child?"

A priest was in the pulpit, still as a carven saint.

"Oh, it's beautiful!" said Smith, ingratiatingly. "Just like me sisters' stories of heaven!"

The priest nodded and smiled kindly.

"What are you looking for, my child?"

"Guidance, Your Reverence," said Smith, who'd decided, this time, to ask roundabout.

"Are you lost?"

"Oh, no, Your Worship! This is 'olborn 'ill!"

The priest compressed his lips and eyed Smith shrewdly. Hurriedly, Smith went on, "Learn me to read, Your 'oliness. That's what I come for. Learn me to read so's I can read the 'oly Scripture."

The priest stared in amazement at the filthy, strong-smelling little creature who stood in the aisle with his black hands pressed to his grubby heart.

"If you come and stand by the door during Service, then you'll hear me reading from the Holy Scripture, child. Won't that be a comfort and help?"

"Oh, yes, Your Grace. And I'm humbly obliged. But what of when I'm 'ome – all in dirt and disorder? Who'll read to me then? And me two poor sisters – a-panting, a-groaning, a-supplicating for salvation? Who'll read to them? Oh, no, Your Reverence – I got to learn to read so's I can comfort meself in the dark o' the night... and light a little lamp in me sisters' souls with perusings aloud from the Good Book!"

But this was too much.

"You're a little liar!" exclaimed the priest, abruptly. Smith gazed thoughtfully up at him, proud in his white surplice and bands.

"And you're a fat bag of rotting flour!" he snarled suddenly. "I 'ope the weevils gets you!"

Was there no one in all the Town who'd teach Smith to read?

He passed the top of Godliman Street. A man came out from somewhere, stopped... and stared at him palely. But Smith, still disheartened by the church's rejection, did not see him and went wearily on.

Smith came to the booksellers in St. Paul's Churchyard. A last hope for the day. And where better to learn to read than in a bookshop?

Several times, he idled up and down, judging his chances in each shop. Here a proprietor scowled at him; there, a clerk shook his fist... and there an entrance was blocked by a fat man who seemed to have died in the act of reading, but came to life to turn a page and acknowledge the helpless bookseller with a corpse-like nod.

But there was one shop that attracted Smith by the mad profusion and tottery architecture of its wares. Books stood in walls and towers and battlements, as if the owner had been in a state of siege for a hundred years – which was partly borne out by his appearance. He was an amazingly thin, wary little man with a nervous affliction which made his head dart from side to side, as if wondering from where the attack might come. Nor was he put at ease when he saw Smith. For he'd seen Smith before – even knew him...

He sat in a curious kind of cave of books where he could jerk and twitch in privacy and quiet.

"Learn us to read, mister!"

"Be off with you!" he said curtly, jerking his head to the right.

"Ain't you got no feelings for your trade?" asked Smith earnestly. "Don't you want it to prosper with more readers –"

"– You're a wicked little thief!" said the bookseller, now jerking to the left.

"– Only because I'm ignorant!"

"Get out of here!"

"*Why* won't you learn me?"

"Keep your thieving hands to yourself!"

"Why won't anybody learn me?"

"Because they've too much sense –"

"– All this goodness and wisdom and learning –" Smith was grandly pointing to the dusty cliffs that reared on either side.

"Touch a book, and I'll finish you!"

The bookseller was now jerking and twitching pretty vigorously and, as his head flew from side to side, Smith considerately tried to keep pace with it – which made him appear as if he was performing a wild dance.

"Keep still!" shouted the bookseller of a sudden – and

jerked worse than ever.

Too late. Smith, capering wider and wider, struck first against one and then against the other of the two tottering shelves.

The calamity that followed, though of brief duration, was terrific in its scope. It was as if the long siege was at last over, and the enemy had breached all the walls at once!

The two walls of shelves had collapsed and with them, brought down in a mighty and thunderous torrent, every last item in the whole of the ramshackle shop!

Books in their fluttering and dusty thousands poured and thumped down as if the very skies had been loaded with them. Histories, Memoirs, Diaries, Lexicons, Grammars, Atlases, Journals, Biographies, Poems, Plays... books about heaven, books about hell, huge books about pygmies, tiny books about giants – even books about books – all, all slid and tumbled into a desperate ruin overhung by a bitter cloud of dust. And somewhere underneath it all, still jerking and twitching, though feebly now, lay the unlucky bookseller himself!

Gawd! thought Smith, halfway around the Cathedral and going like the wind, 'e must be squashed flatter than an old sixpence!

But the bookseller was alive, and while Smith was still running and wondering hopelessly whom next he could ask to teach him to read, his last victim was being exhumed by neighbors and passersby. Strangely enough, he seemed almost the better for the disaster, as though, all his life, he'd expected and dreaded it and now that it had happened, a load was fallen from his soul. He jerked and twitched hardly at all as he told how it had come about and who'd been chiefly to blame.

"They call him Smith," he said.

"And where does he come from?"

"Somewhere near the Ditch. I fancy it's the Red Lion Tavern..."

The questioner had been a passerby: the man who'd earlier come out of Godliman Street.

MR. TOAD ON THE RUN

from

THE WIND IN THE WILLOWS

by

KENNETH GRAHAME

"Mouse" was the nickname given to Kenneth Grahame's small son Alistair, and some time in 1904, Grahame was said by the family's nursemaid to be telling Mouse a serial bedtime story: "Some ditty" (the nursemaid's word for a story) "about a toad." When the story was committed to print and published four years later, to become one of the very great children's classics, it was a story also about a Rat, and a Mole, and a Badger, and about life on the river, as well as being about Mr. Toad of Toad Hall, who maddens his friends by constantly having some wild enthusiasm that in no time at all is replaced by another enthusiasm, equally wild. Most end in disaster, but the disaster leads to a new passion. Owing to a passion for motoring, the rash and conceited Toad can't help trying out someone else's car, without permission, and so ends in jail. Where he might have stayed, but for the jailer's daughter, who grew sorry for him.

Kenneth Grahame lived from 1859 to 1932.

O ne morning, the girl was very thoughtful, and answered at random, and did not seem to Toad to be paying proper attention to his witty sayings and sparkling comments.

"Toad," she said presently, "just listen, please. I have an aunt who is a washerwoman."

"There, there," said Toad graciously and affably, "never mind; think no more about it. *I* have several aunts who *ought* to be washerwomen."

"Do be quiet a minute, Toad," said the girl. "You talk too much, that's your chief fault, and I'm trying to think, and you hurt my head. As I said, I have an aunt who is a washer-woman; she does washing for all the prisoners in this castle – we try to keep any paying business of that sort in the family, you understand. She takes out the washing on Monday morning and brings it in on Friday evening. This is a Thursday. Now, this is what occurs to me: you're very rich – at least, you're always telling me so – and she's very poor. A few pounds wouldn't make any difference to you, and it would mean a lot to her. Now, I think if she were properly approached – squared, I believe, is the word you animals use – you could come to some arrangement by which she would let you have her dress and bonnet and so on, and you could escape from the castle as the official washerwoman. You're very alike in many respects – particularly about the figure."

"We're *not*," said the Toad in a huff. "I have a very elegant figure – for what I am."

"So has my aunt," replied the girl, "for what *she* is. But

have it your own way. You horrid, proud, ungrateful animal, when I'm sorry for you, and trying to help you!"

"Yes, yes, that's all right; thank you very much indeed," said the Toad hurriedly. "But look here! you wouldn't surely have Mr. Toad, of Toad Hall, going about the country disguised as a washerwoman!"

"Then you can stop here as a Toad," replied the girl with much spirit. "I suppose you want to go off in a coach-and-four!"

Honest Toad was always ready to admit himself in the wrong. "You are a good, kind, clever girl," he said, "and I am indeed a proud and stupid toad. Introduce me to your worthy aunt, if you will be so kind, and I have no doubt that the excellent lady and I will be able to arrange terms satisfactory to both parties."

Next evening, the girl ushered her aunt into Toad's cell, bearing his week's washing pinned up in a towel. The old lady had been prepared beforehand for the interview, and the sight of certain gold sovereigns that Toad had thoughtfully placed on the table in full view practically completed the matter and left little further to discuss. In return for his cash, Toad received a cotton print dress, an apron, a shawl, and a rusty black bonnet; the only stipulation the old lady made being that she should be gagged and bound and dumped down in a corner. By this not very convincing artifice, she explained, aided by picturesque fiction which she could supply herself, she hoped to retain her situation, in spite of the suspicious appearance of things.

Toad was delighted with the suggestion. It would enable him to leave the prison in some style, and with his reputation for being a desperate and dangerous fellow untarnished; and he readily helped the jailer's daughter to make her aunt appear as much as possible the victim of circumstances over which she had no control.

"Now it's your turn, Toad," said the girl. "Take off that coat and vest of yours; you're fat enough as it is."

Shaking with laughter, she proceeded to "hook-and-eye" him into the cotton print dress, arranged the shawl with a professional fold, and tied the strings of the rusty bonnet under his chin.

"You're the very image of her," she giggled, "only I'm sure you never looked half so respectable in all your life before. Now, good-bye, Toad, and good luck. Go straight down the way you came up; and if anyone says anything to you, as they probably will, being but men, you can chaff back a bit, of course, but remember you're a widow woman, quite alone in the world, with a character to lose."

With a quaking heart, but as firm a footstep as he could command, Toad set forth cautiously on what seemed to be a most hare-brained and hazardous undertaking; but he was soon agreeably surprised to find how easy everything was made for him, and a little humbled at the thought that both his popularity, and the sex that seemed to inspire it, were really another's. The washerwoman's squat figure in its familiar cotton print seemed a passport for every barred door and grim gateway; even when he hesitated, uncertain as to the right turning to take, he found himself helped out of his difficulty by the warder at the next gate, anxious to be off to his tea, summoning him to come along sharp and not keep him waiting there all night. The chaff and the humorous sallies to which he was subjected, and to which, of course, he had to provide prompt and effective reply, formed, indeed, his chief danger; for Toad was an animal with a strong sense of his own dignity, and the chaff was mostly (he thought) poor and clumsy, and the humor of the sallies entirely lacking. However, he kept his temper, though with great difficulty, suited his retorts to his company and his supposed character, and did his best not to overstep the limits of good taste.

It seemed hours before he crossed the last courtyard, rejected the pressing invitation from the last guardroom, and dodged the outspread arms of the last warder, pleading with simulated passion for just one farewell embrace. But at last, he heard the wicket-gate in the great outer door click behind him, felt the fresh air of the outer world upon his anxious brow, and knew that he was free.

Dizzy with the easy success of his daring exploit, he walked quickly toward the lights of the town, not knowing in the least what he should do next, only quite certain of one thing, that he must remove himself as quickly as possible from a neighborhood where the lady he was forced to represent was so well-known and so popular a character.

As he walked along, considering, his attention was caught by some red and green lights a little way off, to one side of the town, and the sound of puffing and snorting of engines and the banging of shunted trucks fell on his ear. "Aha!" he thought, "this is a piece of luck! A railway station is the thing I want most in the whole world at this moment; and what's more, I needn't go through the town to get to it, and shan't have to support this humiliating character by repartees which, though thoroughly effective, do not assist one's sense of self-respect."

He made his way to the station accordingly, consulted a timetable, and found that a train, bound more or less in the direction of his home, was due to start in half an hour. "More luck!" said Toad, his spirits rising rapidly, and went off to the office to buy his ticket.

He gave the name of the station that he knew to be nearest to the village of which Toad Hall was the principal feature, and mechanically put his fingers, in search of the necessary money, where his vest pocket should have been. But here the cotton dress, which had nobly stood by him so far, and which he had basely forgotten, intervened, and frustrated his efforts. In a sort of nightmare, he struggled with the strange, uncanny thing that seemed to hold his hands, turn all muscular strivings to water, and laugh at him all the time; while other travelers, forming up in a line behind, waited with impatience, making suggestions of more or less value, and comments of more or less stringency and point. At last – somehow – he never rightly understood how – he burst the barriers, attained the goal, arrived at where all vest pockets are eternally situated, and found – not only no money, but no pocket to hold it, and no vest to hold the pocket!

To his horror, he recollected that he had left both coat and vest behind him in his cell, and with them his wallet, money, keys, watch, matches, pencil-case – all that makes life worth living, all that distinguishes the many-pocketed animal, the lord of creation, from the inferior one-pocketed or no-pocketed productions that hop or trip about permissively, unequipped for the real contest.

In his misery, he made one desperate effort to carry the thing off, and, with a return to his fine old manner – a blend of the Squire and the College Professor – he said, "Look here! I find I've left my wallet behind. Just give me the ticket, will you, and I'll send the money on tomorrow. I'm well known in these parts."

The clerk stared at him and the rusty black bonnet a moment, and then laughed. "I should think you were pretty well known in these parts," he said, "if you've tried this game on often. Here, stand away from the window, please, madam; you're obstructing the other passengers!"

An old gentleman who had been prodding him in the back for some moments here thrust him away, and, what was worse, addressed him as his good woman, which angered Toad more than anything that had occurred that evening.

Baffled and full of despair, he wandered blindly down the platform where the train was standing, and tears trickled down each side of his nose. It was hard, he thought, to be within sight of safety and almost of home, and to be baulked by the want of a few wretched shillings and by the pettifogging mistrustfulness of paid officials. Very soon, his escape would be discovered, the hunt would be up, he would be caught, reviled, loaded with chains, dragged back again to prison and bread-and-water and straw; his guards and penalties would be doubled; and O, what sarcastic remarks the girl would make! What was to be done? He was not swift of foot; his figure was unfortunately recognizable. Could he not squeeze under the seat of a carriage? He had seen this method adopted by schoolboys, when the journey-money provided by thoughtful parents had been diverted to other and better ends. As he pondered, he found himself opposite the engine, which was being oiled, wiped, and generally caressed by its affectionate driver, a burly man with an oil can in one hand and a lump of cotton-waste in the other.

"Hullo, mother!" said the engine-driver, "what's the trouble? You don't look particularly cheerful."

"O, sir!" said Toad, crying afresh, "I am a poor, unhappy washerwoman, and I've lost all my money and can't pay for a ticket, and I *must* get home tonight somehow, and whatever I am to do, I don't know. O dear, O dear!"

"That's a bad business, indeed," said the engine driver reflectively. "Lost your money – and can't get home – and got some kids, too, waiting for you, I dare say?"

"Any amount of 'em," sobbed Toad. "And they'll be hungry – and playing with matches – and upsetting lamps, the little innocents! – and quarreling, and going on generally. O dear, O dear!"

"Well, I'll tell you what I'll do," said the good engine-driver. "You're a washerwoman to your trade, says you. Very well, that's that. And I'm an engine-driver, as you may well see, and there's no denying it's terrible dirty work. Uses up a power of shirts, it does, till my missus is fair tired of washing of 'em. If you'll wash a few shirts for me when you get home, and send 'em along, I'll give you a ride on my engine. It's against Company regulations, but we're not so very particular in these out-of-the-way parts."

The Toad's misery turned into rapture as he eagerly scrambled up into the cab of the engine. Of course, he had never washed a shirt in his life, and couldn't if he tried and, anyhow, he wasn't going to begin; but he thought: "When I get safely home to Toad Hall, and have money back again, and pockets to put it in, I will send the engine-driver enough to pay for quite a quantity of washing, and that will be the same thing, or better."

The guard waved his welcome flag, the engine-driver whistled in cheerful response, and the train moved out of the station. As the speed increased, and the Toad could see on either side of him real fields, and trees, and hedges, and cows, and horses, all flying past him, and as he thought how every minute was bringing him nearer to Toad Hall, and sympathetic friends, and money to chink in his pocket, and a soft bed to sleep in, and good things to eat, and praise and admiration at the recital of his adventures and his surpassing cleverness, he began to skip up and down and shout and sing snatches of song, to the great astonishment of the engine-driver, who had come across washerwomen before, at long intervals, but never one at all like this.

They had covered many and many a mile, and Toad was already considering what he would have for supper as soon as he got home, when he noticed that the engine-driver, with a puzzled expression on his face, was leaning over the side of the engine and listening hard. Then he saw him climb onto the coals and gaze out over the top of the train; then he returned and said to Toad: "It's very strange; we're the last train running in this direction tonight, yet I could be sworn that I heard another following us!"

Toad ceased his frivolous antics at once. He became grave and depressed, and a dull pain in the lower part of his spine, communicating itself to his leg, made him want to sit down and try desperately not to think of all the possibilities.

By this time, the moon was shining brightly, and the engine-driver, steadying himself on the coal, could command a view of the line behind them for a long distance.

Presently, he called out, "I can see it clearly now! It is an engine, on our rails, coming along at a great pace! It looks as if we were being pursued!"

The miserable Toad, crouching in the coal-dust, tried hard to think of something to do, with dismal want of success.

"They are gaining on us fast!" cried the engine-driver. "And the engine is crowded with the queerest lot of people! Men like ancient warders, waving halberds; policeman in their helmets, waving truncheons; and shabbily dressed men in pot-hats, obvious and unmistakable plainclothes detectives even at this distance, waving revolvers and walking-sticks; all waving, and all shouting the same thing – 'Stop, stop, stop!'"

Then Toad fell on his knees among the coals and, raising his clasped paw in supplication, cried, "Save me, only save me, dear kind Mr. Engine-driver, and I will confess everything! I am not the simple washerwoman I seem to be! I have no children waiting for me, innocent or otherwise! I am a toad – the well-known and popular Mr. Toad, a landed proprietor; I have just escaped, by my great daring and cleverness, from a loathsome dungeon into which my enemies had flung me; and if those fellows on that engine recapture me, it will be chains and bread-and-water and straw and misery once more for poor, unhappy, innocent Toad!"

The engine-driver looked down upon him very sternly, and said, "Now, tell the truth; what were you put in prison for?"

"It was nothing very much," said poor Toad, coloring deeply. "I only borrowed a motorcar while the owners were at lunch; they had no need of it at the time. I didn't mean to steal it, really; but people – especially magistrates – take such harsh views of thoughtless and high-spirited actions."

The engine-driver looked very grave and said, "I fear that you have indeed been a wicked toad, and by rights I ought to give you up to offended justice. But you are evidently in sore trouble and distress, so I will not desert you. I don't hold with motorcars, for one thing; and I don't hold with being ordered about by policeman when I'm on my own engine, for another. And the sight of an animal in tears always makes me feel queer and softhearted. So cheer up, Toad! I'll do my best, and we may beat them yet!"

They piled on more coals, shoveling furiously; the furnace roared, the sparks flew, the engine leapt and swung, but still their pursuers slowly gained. The engine-driver, with a sigh, wiped his brow with a handful of cotton-waste, and said, "I'm afraid it's no good, Toad. You see, they are running light, and they have the better engine. There's only one thing left for us to do, and it's your only chance, so attend very carefully to what I tell you. A short way ahead of us is a long tunnel, and on the other side of that the line passes through thick woods. Now, I will put on all the speed I can while we are running through the tunnel, but the other fellows will slow down a bit, naturally, for fear of an accident. When we are through, I will shut off steam and put on the brakes as hard as I can, and the moment it's safe to do so, you must jump and hide in the woods, before they get through the tunnel and see you. Then I will go at full speed ahead again, and they can chase *me* if they like, for as long as they like, and as far as they like. Now mind, and be ready to jump when I tell you!"

They piled on more coals, and the train shot into the tunnel, and the engine rushed and roared and rattled, till at last they shot out at the other end into fresh air and the peaceful moonlight, and saw the woods lying dark and helpful upon both sides of the line. The driver shut off the steam and put on the brakes, the Toad got down on the step, and as the train slowed down to almost a walking pace, he heard the driver call out, "Now, jump!"

Toad jumped, rolled down a short embankment, picked himself up unhurt, scrambled into the woods, and hid.

Peeping out, he saw his train get up speed again and disappear at a great pace. Then out of the tunnel burst the pursuing engine, roaring and whistling, her motley crew waving their various weapons and shouting, "Stop! stop! stop!" When they were past, the Toad had a hearty laugh – for the first time since he was thrown into prison.

But he soon stopped laughing when he came to consider that it was now very late and dark and cold, and he was in an unknown wood, with no money and no chance of supper, and still far from friends and home; and the dead silence of everything, after the roar and rattle of the train, was something of a shock. He dared not leave the shelter of the trees, so he struck into the woods, with the idea of leaving the railroad as far as possible behind him.

After so many weeks within walls, he found the woods strange and unfriendly and inclined, he thought, to make fun of him. Night-jars, sounding their mechanical rattle, made him think that the wood was full of searching warders, closing in on him. An owl, swooping noiselessly toward him, brushed his shoulder with its wing, making him jump with the horrid certainty that it was a hand; then flitted off, moth-like, laughing its low ho! ho! ho! which Toad thought in very poor taste. Once he met a fox, who stopped, looked him up and down in a sarcastic sort of way, and said, "Hullo, washerwoman! Half a pair of socks and a pillowcase short this week! Mind it doesn't happen again!" and swaggered off, sniggering. Toad looked about for a stone to throw at him, but could not succeed in finding one, which vexed him more than anything. At last, cold, hungry, and tired out, he sought the shelter of a hollow tree, where with branches and dead leaves, he made himself as comfortable a bed as he could and slept soundly till the morning.

THE INVISIBLE CHILD

from
TALES FROM MOOMIN VALLEY

by
TOVE JANSSON

There are, basically, Moominpappa, Moominmamma, their son Moomintroll and Little My, who is startlingly naughty. The Moomins used to be trolls, hairy, nasty-natured, and nocturnal: now they're friendly animals, each like a sort of small, round hippopotamus, loving the sun and the daylight, but sleeping solidly from November till Spring. They have neighbors and friends as odd and enchanting as themselves, including the Hemulens (a sort of sad Moomins), the wholly mysterious Snorks, and the Hattifatteners, who are extremely difficult to describe: you might say that they were a kind of walking candle. Too-Ticky is a winter visitor who camps in the bathhouse, and the Groke is a silent creature who freezes everything and everyone she touches.

Tove Jansson, born in 1914, comes from Finland and writes in Swedish. There are many Moomin books: the first, Comet in Moominland, *was published in 1946.*

O ne dark and rainy evening, the Moomin family sat around the veranda table picking over the day's mushroom harvest. The big table was covered with newspapers, and in the center of it stood the lighted kerosene lamp. But the corners of the veranda were dark.

"My has been picking pepper spunk again," Moominpappa said. "Last year, she collected flybane."

"Let's hope she takes to chanterelles next fall," said Moominmamma. "Or at least to something not directly poisonous."

"Hope for the best and prepare for the worst," little My observed with a chuckle.

They continued their work in peaceful silence.

Suddenly, there were a few light taps on the glass pane in the door, and without waiting for an answer, Too-ticky came in and shook the rain off her oilskin jacket. Then she held the door open and called out in the dark: "Well, come along!"

"Whom are you bringing?" Moomintroll asked.

"It's Ninny," Too-ticky said. "Yes, her name's Ninny."

She still held the door open, waiting. No one came.

"Oh, well," Too-ticky said and shrugged her shoulders. "If she's too shy, she'd better stay there for a while."

"She'll be drenched through," said Moominmamma.

"Perhaps that won't matter much when one's invisible," Too-ticky said and sat down by the table. The family stopped working and waited for an explanation.

"You all know, don't you, that if people are frightened very often, they sometimes become invisible," Too-ticky said and swallowed a small egg mushroom that looked like a little snowball. "Well. This Ninny was frightened the wrong way by a lady who had taken care of her without really liking her. I've met this lady, and she was horrid. Not the angry sort, you know, which would have been understandable. No, she was the icily ironical kind."

"What's ironical?" Moomintroll asked.

"Well, imagine that you slip on a rotten mushroom and sit down on the basket of newly picked ones," Too-ticky said. "The natural thing for your mother would be to be angry. But no, she isn't. Instead she says, very coldly: 'I understand that's your idea of a graceful dance, but I'd thank you not to do it in people's food.' Something like that."

"How unpleasant," Moomintroll said.

"Yes, isn't it," replied Too-ticky. "This was the way this lady used to talk. She was ironic all day long every day, and finally the kid started to turn pale and fade around the edges, and less and less was seen of her. Last Friday, one couldn't catch sight of her at all. The lady gave her away to me and said she really couldn't take care of relatives she couldn't even see."

"And what did you do to the lady?" My asked with bulging eyes. "Did you bash her head?"

"That's of no use with the ironic sort," Too-ticky said. "I took Ninny home with me, of course. And now I've brought her here for you to make her visible again."

There was a slight pause. Only the rain was heard, rustling along over the veranda roof. Everybody stared at Too-ticky and thought for a while.

"Does she talk?" Moominpappa asked.

"No. But the lady has hung a small silver bell around her neck so that one can hear where she is."

Too-ticky arose and opened the door again. "Ninny!" she called out in the dark.

The cool smell of fall crept in from the yard and a square of light threw itself on the wet grass. After a while, there was a slight tinkle outside, rather hesitantly. The sound came up the steps and stopped. A bit above the floor, a small silver bell was seen hanging in the air on a black ribbon. Ninny seemed to have a very thin neck.

"All right," Too-ticky said. "Now, here's your new family. They're a bit silly at times, but rather decent, largely speaking."

"Give the kid a chair," Moominpappa said. "Does she know how to pick mushrooms?"

"I really know nothing at all about Ninny," Too-ticky said, "I've only brought her here and told you what I know. Now, I have a few other things to attend to. Please look in some day, won't you, and let me know how you get along. Cheerio."

When Too-ticky had gone, the family sat quite silent, looking at the empty chair and the silver bell. After a while, one of the chanterelles slowly rose from the heap on the table. Invisible paws picked it clean from needles and earth. Then it was cut to pieces, and the pieces drifted away and laid themselves in the basin. Another mushroom sailed up from the table.

"Thrilling!" My said with awe. "Try to give her something to eat. I'd like to know if you can see the food when she swallows it."

"How on earth does one make her visible again?" Moominpappa said worriedly. "Should we take her to a doctor?"

"I don't think so," said Moominmamma. "I believe she wants to be invisible for a while. Too-ticky said she's shy. Better to leave the kid alone until something turns up."

And so it was decided.

The eastern attic room happened to be unoccupied, so Moominmamma made Ninny a bed there. The silver bell tinkled along after her upstairs and reminded Moominmamma of the cat that once had lived with them. At the bedside, she laid out the apple, the glass of juice, and the three striped pieces of candy everybody in the house was given at bedtime.

Then she lit a candle and said:

"Now, have a good sleep, Ninny. Sleep as late as you can. There'll be tea for you in the morning, any time you want. And if you happen to get a funny feeling or if you want anything, just come downstairs and tinkle."

Moominmamma saw the quilt raise itself to form a very small mound. A dent appeared in the pillow. She went downstairs again to her own room and started looking through her granny's old notes about Infallible Household Remedies. Evil Eye. Melancholy. Colds. No. There didn't seem to be anything suitable. Yes, there was. Toward the end of the notebook, she found a few lines written down at the time when Granny's hand was already rather shaky. "If people start getting misty and difficult to see." Good. Moominmamma read the recipe, which was rather complicated, and started at once to mix the medicine for little Ninny.

The bell came tinkling downstairs, one step at a time, with a small pause between each step. Moomintroll had waited for it all morning. But the silver bell wasn't the exciting thing. That was the paws. Ninny's paws were coming down the steps. They were very small, with anxiously bunched toes. Nothing else of Ninny was visible. It was very odd.

Moomintroll drew back behind the porcelain stove and stared bewitchedly at the paws that passed him on their way to the veranda. Now she served herself some tea. The cup was raised in the air and sank back again. She ate some bread and butter and marmalade. Then the cup and saucer drifted away to the kitchen, were washed, and put away in the closet. You see, Ninny was a very orderly little child.

Moomintroll rushed out in the garden and shouted: "Mamma! She's got paws! You can see her paws!"

I thought as much, Moominmamma was thinking where she sat high in the apple tree. Granny knew a thing or two. Now, when the medicine starts to work, we'll be on the right way.

"Splendid," said Moominpappa. "And better still when she shows her snout one day. It makes me feel sad to talk with people who are invisible. And who never answer me."

"Hush, dear," Moominmamma said warningly. Ninny's paws were standing in the grass among the fallen apples.

"Hello, Ninny," shouted My. "You've slept like a hog. When are you going to show your snout? You must look a fright if you've wanted to be invisible."

"Shut up," Moomintroll whispered, "she'll be hurt." He went running up to Ninny and said:

"Never mind My. She's hardboiled. You're really safe here among us. Don't even think about that horrid lady. She can't come here and take you away..."

In a moment, Ninny's paws had faded away and become nearly indistinguishable from the grass.

"Darling, you're an idiot," said Moominmamma. "You can't go about reminding the kid about those things. Now pick apples and don't talk nonsense."

They all picked apples.

After a while, Ninny's paws became clearer again and climbed one of the trees.

It was a beautiful fall morning. The shadows made one's snout a little chilly, but the sunshine felt nearly like summer. Everything was wet from the night's rain, and all colors were strong and clear. When all the apples were picked or shaken down, Moominpappa carried the biggest apple mincer out in the yard, and they started making applesauce.

Moomintroll turned the handle, Moominmamma fed the mincer with apples, and Moominpappa carried the filled jars to the veranda. Little My sat in a tree singing the Big Apple song.

Suddenly, there was a crash.

On the garden path appeared a large heap of applesauce, all prickly with glass splinters. Beside the heap, one could see Ninny's paws, rapidly fading away.

"Oh," said Moominmamma. "That was the jar we use to give to the bumblebees. Now, we needn't carry it down to the field. And Granny always said that if you want the earth to grow something for you, then you have to give it a present in the fall."

Ninny's paws appeared back again, and above them a pair of spindly legs came to view. Above the legs, one could see the faint outline of a brown dress hem.

"I can see her legs!" cried Moomintroll.

"Congrats," said little My, looking down out of her tree. "Not bad. But the Groke knows why you must wear snuff-brown."

Moominmamma nodded to herself and sent a thought to her Granny and the medicine.

Ninny padded along after them all day. They became used to the tinkle and no longer thought Ninny very remarkable.

By evening, they had nearly forgotten about her. But when everybody was in bed, Moominmamma took out a rose-pink shawl of hers and made it into a little dress.

When it was ready, she carried it upstairs to the eastern attic room and cautiously laid it out on a chair. Then she made a broad hair ribbon out of the material left over.

Moominmamma was enjoying herself tremendously. It was exactly like sewing doll's clothes again. And the funny thing was that one didn't know if the doll had yellow or black hair.

The following day, Ninny had her dress on. She was visible up to her neck, and when she came down to morning tea, she bobbed and piped:

"Thank you all ever so much."

The family felt very embarrassed, and no one found anything to say. Also it was hard to know where to look when one talked to Ninny. Of course, one tried to look a bit above the bell where Ninny was supposed to have her eyes. But then, very easily, one found oneself staring at some of the visible things further down instead, and it gave one an impolite feeling.

Moominpappa cleared his throat. "We're happy to see," he started, "that we see more of Ninny today. The more we see, the happier we are..."

My gave a laugh and banged the table with her spoon. "Fine that you've started talking," she said. "Hope you have anything to say. Do you know any good games?"

"No," Ninny piped. "But I've heard about games."

Moomintroll was delighted. He decided to teach Ninny all the games he knew.

After coffee, all three of them went down to the river to play. Only Ninny turned out to be quite impossible. She bobbed and nodded and very seriously replied, quite, and how funny, and of course, but it was clear to all that she played only from politeness and not to have fun.

"Run, run, can't you!" My cried. "Or can't you even jump?"

Ninny's thin legs dutifully ran and jumped. Then she stood still again with arms dangling. The empty dress neck over the bell was looking strangely helpless.

"D'you think anybody likes that?" My cried. "Haven't you any life in you? D'you want a biff on the nose?"

"Rather not," Ninny piped humbly.

"She can't play," mumbled Moomintroll.

"She can't get angry," little My said. "That's what's wrong with her. Listen, you," My continued and went close to Ninny with a menacing look. "You'll never have a face of your own until you've learned to fight. Believe me."

"Yes, of course," Ninny replied, cautiously backing away.

There was no further turn for the better.

At last, they stopped trying to teach Ninny to play. She didn't like funny stories either. She never laughed at the right places. She never laughed at all, in fact. This had a depressing effect on the person who told the story. And she was left alone to herself.

Days went by, and Ninny was still without a face. They became accustomed to seeing her pink dress marching along behind Moominmamma. As soon as Moominmamma stopped, the silver bell also stopped, and when she continued her way, the bell began tinkling again. A bit above the dress a big rose-pink bow was bobbing in thin air.

Moominmamma continued to treat Ninny with Granny's medicine, but nothing further happened. So, after some time, she stopped the treatment, thinking that many people had managed all right before without a head, and besides perhaps Ninny wasn't very good-looking.

Now everyone could imagine for himself what she looked like, and this can often brighten up a relationship.

One day, the family went off through the woods down to the beach. They were going to pull the boat up for winter. Ninny came tinkling behind as usual, but when they came in view of the sea, she suddenly stopped. Then she lay down on her stomach in the sand and started to whine.

"What's come over Ninny? Is she frightened?" asked Moominpappa.

"Perhaps she hasn't seen the sea before," Moominmamma said. She stooped and exchanged a few whispering words with Ninny. Then she straightened up again and said:

"No, it's the first time. Ninny thinks the sea's too big."

"Of all the silly kids," little My started, but Moominmamma gave her a severe look and said: "Don't be a silly kid yourself. Now let's pull the boat ashore."

They went out on the dock to the bathhouse where Tooticky lived and knocked at the door.

"Hullo," Too-ticky said, "how's the invisible child?"

"There's only her snout left," Moominpappa replied. "At the moment, she's a bit startled, but it'll pass over. Can you lend us a hand with the boat?"

"Certainly," Too-ticky said.

While the boat was pulled ashore and turned keel upward Ninny had padded down to the water's edge and was standing immobile on the wet sand. They left her alone.

Moominmamma sat down on the dock and looked down into the water. "Dear me, how cold it looks," she said. And then she yawned a bit and added that nothing exciting had happened for weeks.

Moominpappa gave Moomintroll a wink, pulled a horrible face, and started to sneak up on Moominmamma from behind.

Of course, he didn't really think of pushing her in the water as he had done many times when she was young. Perhaps he didn't even want to startle her, but just to amuse the kids a little.

But before he reached her, a sharp cry was heard, a pink streak of lightning shot over the dock, and Moominpappa let out a scream and dropped his hat into the water. Ninny had sunk her small, invisible teeth in Moominpappa's tail, and they were sharp.

"Good work!" cried My. "I couldn't have done it better myself!"

Ninny was standing on the dock. She had a small, snub-nosed, angry face below a red tangle of hair. She was hissing at Moominpappa like a cat.

"Don't you *dare* push her into the big, horrible sea!" she cried.

"I see her, I see her!" shouted Moomintroll. "She's sweet!"

"Sweet, my eye," said Moominpappa, inspecting his bitten tail. "She's the silliest, nastiest, badly-brought-uppest child I've ever seen, with or without a head."

He knelt down on the dock and tried to fish for his hat with a stick. And in some mysterious way, he managed to tip himself over and tumbled in on his head.

He came up at once, standing safely on the bottom, with his snout above water and his ears filled with mud.

"Oh, dear!" Ninny was shouting, "Oh, how great! Oh, how funny!"

The dock shook with her laughter.

"I believe she's never laughed before," Too-ticky said wonderingly. "You seem to have changed her, she's even worse than little My. But the main thing is that one can see her, of course."

"It's all thanks to Granny," Moominmamma said.

TOM'S MONDAY MORNING

from

THE ADVENTURES OF TOM SAWYER

by

MARK TWAIN

In Tom Sawyer, *Mark Twain looked back on the days of his own childhood on the banks of the Mississippi, in the 1840s: a rough, tough, marvelous world, dominated by the wide river. Tom is a willful boy, with an imagination that runs away with him more often than not. Tom's closest friend is Huck Finn, who was to become the hero of* The Adventures of Huckleberry Finn, *the sequel to* Tom Sawyer. *Abandoned by his drunken father, Huck lives the life of an outcast and wouldn't swap his barrel, his idle days, and his freedom to smoke and swear for all the schools and respectable homes in existence. The boys of the village*

are forbidden to associate with him and so, of course, are very keen to do so. The main story in Tom Sawyer *tells (with moments of sheer terror) of Tom and Huck's involvement with the murderous Injun Joe.*

Mark Twain, whose real name was Samuel Clemens, lived from 1835 to 1910: apprenticed first to a printer, he became a Mississippi River pilot (where he picked up the name "Mark Twain": it was one of the cries shouted when a marked line was lowered into the water to measure its depth) and a newspaper reporter before becoming, simply, one of the most famous writers of his time.

Monday morning found Tom Sawyer miserable. Monday morning always found him so – because it began another week's slow suffering in school. He generally began that day with wishing he had had no intervening holiday, it made the going into captivity and fetters again so much more odious.

Tom lay thinking. Presently it occurred to him that he wished he was sick; then he could stay home from school. Here was a vague possibility. He canvassed his system. No ailment was found, and he investigated again. This time, he thought he could detect colicky symptoms, and he began to encourage them with considerable hope. But they soon grew feeble, and presently died wholly away. He reflected further. Suddenly he discovered something. One of his upper front teeth was loose. This was lucky; he was about to begin to groan as a "starter," as he called it, when it occurred to him that if he came into court with that argument, his aunt would pull it out, and that would hurt. So he thought he would hold the tooth in reserve for the present, and seek further. Nothing offered for some little time, and then he remembered hearing the doctor tell about a certain thing that laid up a patient for two or three weeks and threatened to make him lose a finger. So the boy eagerly drew his sore toe from under the sheet and held it up for inspection. But now he did not know the necessary symptoms. However, it seemed well worthwhile to chance it, so he fell to groaning with considerable spirit.

But Sid slept on unconscious.

Tom groaned louder and fancied that he began to feel pain in the toe.

No result from Sid.

Tom was panting with his exertions by this time. He took a rest and then swelled himself up and fetched a succession of admirable groans.

Sid snored on.

Tom was aggravated. He said, "Sid, Sid!" and shook him. This course worked well, and Tom began to groan again. Sid yawned, stretched, then brought himself up on his elbow with a snort, and began to stare at Tom. Tom went on groaning. Sid said:

"Tom! Say, Tom!" (No response.) "Here, Tom! *Tom*! What is the matter, Tom?" And he shook him and looked in his face anxiously.

Tom moaned out:

"Oh, don't Sid. Don't joggle me."

"Why, what's the matter, Tom? I must call Auntie."

"No – never mind. It'll be over by and by, maybe. Don't call anybody."

"But I must! *Don't* groan so, Tom, it's awful. How long you been this way?"

"Hours. Ouch! Oh, don't stir so, Sid, you'll kill me."

"Tom, why didn't you wake me sooner? Oh, Tom, *don't*! It makes my flesh crawl to hear you. Tom, what *is* the matter?"

"I forgive you everything, Sid. (Groan.) Everything you've ever done to me. When I'm gone –"

"Oh, Tom, you ain't dying are you? Don't, Tom – oh, don't. Maybe –"

"I forgive everybody, Sid. (Groan.) Tell 'em so, Sid. And, Sid, you give my window sash and my cat with one eye to that new girl that's come to town, and tell her –"

But Sid had snatched his clothes and gone. Tom was suffering in reality, now, so handsomely was his imagination working, and so his groans had gathered quite a genuine tone.

Sid flew downstairs and said:

"Oh, Aunt Polly, come! Tom's dying!"

"Dying!"

"Yes'm. Don't wait – come quick!"

"Rubbage! I don't believe it!"

But she fled upstairs, nevertheless, with Sid and Mary at her heels. And her face grew white, too, and her lip trembled. When she reached the bedside, she gasped out:

"You, Tom! Tom, what's the matter with you?"

"Oh, Auntie, I'm –"

"What's the matter with you, child?"

"Oh, Auntie, my sore toe's mortified!"

The old lady sank down into a chair and laughed a little, then cried a little, then did both together. This restored her, and she said:

"Tom, what a turn you did give me. Now you shut up that nonsense and climb out of this."

The groans ceased, and the pain vanished from the toe. The boy felt a little foolish, and he said:

"Aunt Polly, it *seemed* mortified, and it hurt so I never minded my tooth at all."

"Your tooth indeed! What's the matter with your tooth?"

"One of them's loose, and it aches perfectly awful."

"There, there, now, don't begin that groaning again. Open your mouth. Well – your tooth *is* loose, but you're not going to die about that. Mary, get me a silk thread, and a chunk of fire out of the kitchen."

Tom said:

"Oh, please, Auntie, don't pull it out. It don't hurt any more. I wish I may never stir if it does. Please don't, Auntie. I don't want to stay home from school."

"Oh, you don't, don't you? So all this row was because you thought you'd get to stay home from school and go a-fishing? Tom, Tom, I love you so, and you seem to try every way you can to break my old heart with your outrageousness." By this time, the dental instruments were ready. The old lady made one end of the silk thread fast to Tom's tooth with a loop and tied the other to the bedpost. Then she seized the chunk of fire and suddenly thrust it almost into the boy's face. The tooth hung dangling by the bedpost, now.

But all trials bring their compensations. As Tom wended to school after breakfast, he was the envy of every boy he met because the gap in his upper row of teeth enabled him to expectorate in a new and admirable way. He gathered quite a following of lads interested in the exhibition; and one that had cut his finger and had been a center of fascination and homage up to this time now found himself suddenly without an adherent and shorn of his glory. His heart was heavy, and he said with a disdain which he did not feel, that it wasn't anything to spit like Tom Sawyer; but another boy said, "Sour grapes!" and he wandered away a dismantled hero.

Shortly Tom came upon the juvenile pariah of the village, Huckleberry Finn, son of the town drunkard. Huckleberry was cordially hated and dreaded by all the mothers of the town, because he was idle and lawless and vulgar and bad – and because all their children admired him so, and delighted in his forbidden society, and wished they dared to be like him. Tom was like the rest of the respectable boys, in that he envied Huckleberry his gaudy outcast condition and was under strict orders not to play with him. So he played with him every time he got a chance. Huckleberry was always dressed in the castoff clothes of full-grown men, and they were in perennial bloom and fluttering with rags. His hat was a vast ruin with a wide crescent lopped out of its brim; his coat, when he wore one, hung nearly to his heels and had the rearward buttons far down the back; but one suspender supported his pants; the seat of the pants bagged low and contained nothing; the fringed legs dragged in the dirt when not rolled up.

Huckleberry came and went of his own free will. He slept on doorsteps in fine weather and in empty hogsheads in wet; he did not have to go to school or church, or call any being master or obey anybody; he could go fishing or swimming when and where he chose, and stay as long as it suited him; nobody forbade him to fight; he could sit up as late as he pleased; he was always the first boy that went barefoot in the spring and the last to resume leather in the fall; he never had to wash, nor put on clean clothes; he could swear wonderfully. In a word, everything that goes to make life precious that boy had. So thought every harassed, hampered, respectable boy in St. Petersburg.

Tom hailed the romantic outcast:

"Hello, Huckleberry!"

"Hello, yourself, and see how you like it."

"What's that you got?"

"Dead cat."

"Lemme see him, Huck. My, he's pretty stiff. Where'd you get him?"

"Bought him off'n a boy."

"What did you give?"

"I give a blue ticket and a bladder that I got at the

slaughterhouse."

"Where'd you get the blue ticket?"

"Bought it off'n Ben Rogers two weeks ago for a hoop-stick."

"Say – what is dead cats good for, Huck?"

"Good for? Cure warts with."

"No! Is that so? I know something that's better."

"I bet you don't. What is it?"

"Why, spunk water."

"Spunk water! I wouldn't give a dern for spunk water."

"You wouldn't, wouldn't you? D'you ever try it?"

"No, I hain't. But Bob Tanner did. He took and dipped his hand in a rotten stump where the rainwater was."

"In the daytime?"

"Certainly."

"With his face to the stump?"

"Yes. Least I reckon so."

"Did he *say* anything?"

"I don't reckon he did. I don't know."

"Aha! Talk about trying to cure warts with spunk water such a blame-fool way as that! Why, that ain't a-going to do any good. You got to go all by yourself, to the middle of the woods, where you know there's a spunk-water stump, and just as it's midnight, you back up against the stump and jam your hand in and say:

> '*Barley-corn, barley-corn, Injun-meal shorts,*
> *Spunk water, spunk water, swaller these warts,*'

and then walk away quick, eleven steps, with your eyes shut, and then turn around three times and walk home without speaking to anybody. Because if you speak, the charm's busted."

"Well, that sounds like a good way; but that ain't the way Bob Tanner done."

"No, sir, you can bet he didn't, becuz he's the wartiest boy in this town; and he wouldn't have a wart on him if he'd knowed how to work spunk water. I've took off thousands of warts off my hands that way. Huck, I play with frogs so much that I've always got considerable many warts. Sometimes I take 'em off with a bean."

"Yes, bean's good. I've done that."

"Have you? What's your way?"

"You take and split the bean, and cut the wart so as to get some blood, and then you put the blood on one piece of the bean, and take and dig a hole and bury it, 'bout midnight at the crossroads in the dark of the moon, and then you burn up the rest of the bean. You see, that piece that's got the blood on it will keep drawing and drawing, trying to fetch the other piece to it, and so that helps the blood to draw the wart, and pretty soon off she comes."

"Yes, that's it, Huck – that's it, though when you're burying it if you say, 'Down bean; off wart: come no more to bother me!' it's better. That's the way Joe Harper does, and he's been nearly to Coonville and most everywheres. But say – how do you cure 'em with dead cats?"

"Why, you take your cat and go and get in the graveyard 'long about midnight when somebody that was wicked has been buried; and when it's midnight a devil will come, or maybe two or three, but you can't see 'em, you can only hear something like the wind, or maybe hear 'em talk; and when they're taking that feller away, you heave your cat after 'em and say, 'Devil follow corpse, cat follow devil, warts follow cat, I'm done with ye!' That'll fetch *any* wart."

"Sound's right. D'you ever try it, Huck?"

"No, but old Mother Hopkins told me."

"Well, I reckon it's so then. Becuz they say she's a witch."

"Say! Why, Tom, I *know* she is. She witched Pap. Pap says so his own self. He come along one day, and he sees she was a-witching him, so he took up a rock, and if she hadn't dodged, he'd 'a' got her. Well, that very night, he rolled off'n a shed wher' he was alayin' drunk and broke his arm."

"Why, that's awful. How did he know she was a-witching him?"

"Lord, Pap can, tell, easy. Pap says when they keep looking at you right stiddy, they're a-witching you. 'Specially if they mumble. Becuz when they mumble, they're saying the Lord's Prayer backards."

"Say, Hucky, when you going to try the cat?"

"Tonight. I reckon they'll come after old Hoss Williams tonight."

"But they buried him Saturday. Didn't they get him Saturday night?"

"Why, how you talk! How could their charms work till midnight? – and *then* it's Sunday. Devils don't slosh around much of a Sunday, I don't reckon."

"I never thought of that. That's so. Lemme go with you?"

"Of course – if you ain't afeard."

"Afeard! 'Tain't likely. Will you meow?"

"Yes – and you meow back, if you get a chance. Last time, you kep' me a-meowing around till old Hays went to throwing rocks at me and says 'Dern that cat!' and so I hove a brick through his window – but don't you tell."

"I won't. I couldn't meow that night becuz Auntie was watching me, but I'll meow this time. Say – what's that?"

"Nothing but a tick."

"Where'd you get him?"

"Out in the woods!"

"What'll you take for him?"

"I don't know. I don't want to sell him."

"All right. It's a mighty small tick anyway."

"Oh, anybody can run a tick down that don't belong to them. I'm satisfied with it. It's a good enough tick for me."

"Sho, there's ticks a-plenty. I could have a thousand of 'em if I wanted to."

"Well, why don't you? Becuz you know mighty well you can't. This is a pretty early tick, I reckon. It's the first one I've seen this year."

"Say, Huck – I'll give you my tooth for him."

"Le's see it."

Tom got out a bit of paper and carefully unrolled it. Huckleberry viewed it wistfully. The temptation was very strong. At last he said:

"Is it genuwyne?"

Tom lifted his lip and showed the vacancy.

"Well, all right," said Huckleberry, "it's a trade."

Tom enclosed the tick in the percussion-cap box that had lately been the pinch bug's prison, and the boys separated, each feeling wealthier than before.

When Tom reached the little isolated frame schoolhouse, he strode in briskly, with the manner of one who had come with all honest speed. He hung his hat on a peg and flung himself into his seat with businesslike alacrity. The master, throned on high in his great splint-bottom armchair, was dozing, lulled by the drowsy hum of study. The interruption roused him.

"Thomas Sawyer!"

Tom knew that when his name was pronounced in full, it meant trouble.

"Sir!"

"Come up here. Now, sir, why are you late again, as usual?"

Tom was about to take refuge in a lie, when he saw two long tails of yellow hair hanging down a back that he recognized by the electric sympathy of love; and by that form was *the only vacant place* on the girls' side of the schoolhouse. He instantly said:

"I STOPPED TO TALK WITH HUCKLEBERRY FINN."

The master's pulse stood still, and he stared helplessly. The buzz of study ceased. The pupils wondered if this foolhardy boy had lost his mind. The master said:

"You – you did what?"

"Stopped to talk with Huckleberry Finn."

There was no mistaking the words.

"Thomas Sawyer, this is the most astounding confession I have ever listened to. No mere ferule will answer for this offence. Take off your jacket."

The master's arm performed until it was tired and the stock of switches notably diminished. Then the order followed:

"Now, sir, go and sit with the *girls!* And let this be a warning to you."

The titter that rippled around the room appeared to abash the boy, but in reality that result was caused rather more by his worshipful awe of his unknown idol and the dread pleasure that lay in his high good fortune. He sat down upon the end of the pine bench and the girl hitched herself away from him with a toss of her head. Nudges and winks and whispers traversed the room, but Tom sat still, with his arms upon the long, low desk before him and seemed to study his book.

By and by, attention ceased from him, and the accustomed school murmur rose upon the dull air once more. Presently, the boy began to steal furtive glances at the girl. She observed it, "made a mouth" at him and gave him the back of her head for the space of a minute. When she cautiously faced around again, a peach lay before her. She thrust it away. Tom gently put it back. She thrust it away again, but with less animosity. Tom patiently returned it to its place.

Then she let it remain. Tom scrawled on his slate, *"Please take it – I got more."* The girl glanced at the words, but made no sign. Now the boy began to draw something on the slate, hiding his work with his left hand. For a time, the girl refused to notice, but her human curiosity presently began to manifest itself by hardly perceptible signs. The boy worked on, apparently unconscious. The girl made a sort of noncommittal attempt to see it, but the boy did not betray that he was aware of it. At last, she gave in and hesitatingly whispered:

"Let me see it."

Tom partly uncovered a dismal caricature of a house with two gable ends to it and a corkscrew of smoke issuing from the chimney. Then the girl's interest began to fasten itself upon the work, and she forgot everything else. When it was finished, she gazed a moment, then whispered:

"It's nice – make a man."

The artist erected a man in the front yard, that resembled a derrick. He could have stepped over the house; but the girl was not hypercritical; she was satisfied with the monster and whispered:

"It's a beautiful man – now make me coming along."

Tom drew an hourglass with a full moon and straw limbs to it and armed the spreading fingers with a portentous fan. The girl said:

"It's ever so nice – I wish I could draw."

"It's easy," whispered Tom, "I'll learn you."

"Oh, will you? When?"

"At noon. Do you go home to dinner?"

"I'll stay if you will."

"Good – that's a whack. What's your name?"

"Becky Thatcher. What's yours? Oh, I know, it's Thomas Sawyer."

"That's the name they lick me by. I'm Tom when I'm good. You call me Tom, will you?"

"Yes."

Now Tom began to scrawl something on the slate, hiding the words from the girl. But she was not backward this time. She begged to see. Tom said:

"Oh, it ain't anything."

"Yes, it is."

"No, it ain't. You don't want to see."

"Yes, I do, indeed I do. Please let me."

"You'll tell."

"No, I won't – 'deed and 'deed and double 'deed I won't."

"You won't tell anybody at all? Ever, as long as you live?"

"No, I won't ever tell *any*body. Now let me."

"Oh, *you* don't want to see!"

"Now that you treat me so, I *will* see." And she put her small hand upon his, and a little scuffle ensued. Tom pretending to resist in earnest, but letting his hand slip by degrees till these words were revealed: *"I love you."*

"Oh, you bad thing!" And she hit his hand a smart rap, but reddened and looked pleased, nevertheless.

Just at this juncture, the boy felt a slow, fateful grip closing on his ear, and a steady lifting impulse. In that vice, he was borne across the house and deposited in his own seat, under a peppering fire of giggles from the whole school. Then the master stood over him during a few awful moments and finally moved away to his throne without saying a word. But although Tom's ear tingled, his heart was jubilant.

As the school quieted down, Tom made an honest effort to study, but the turmoil within him was too great. In turn, he took his place in the reading class and made a botch of it; then in the geography class and turned lakes into mountains, mountains into rivers, and rivers into continents, till chaos was come again; then in the spelling class, and got "turned down" by a succession of mere baby words till he brought up at the foot and yielded up the pewter medal which he had worn with ostentation for months.

HORROR IN THE PIT

from
THE PIT AND THE PENDULUM

by
EDGAR ALLAN POE

In The Pit and the Pendulum, *the narrator has been condemned (by monks) to a curiously horrible slow death. This story has the extraordinary atmosphere common to much of Edgar Allan Poe's writing – like that of a nightmare, but very clear and intense in detail. It is a story for those who enjoy being terrified.*

Poe, who lived from 1809 to 1849, was a remarkable poet (his best-known poem is The Raven*): and he was also one of the earliest writers of detective fiction – you should look for* The Murders in the Rue Morgue *and* The Mystery of Marie Roget. *Among his other hair-raising stories are* The Gold Bug *(the best of all stories about the solving of a coded message or cryptogram) and* The Fall of the House of Usher.

U pon arousing, I found by my side, as before, a loaf and a pitcher of water, a burning thirst consumed me, and I emptied the vessel at a draft. It must have been drugged; for scarcely had I drunk, before I became irresistibly drowsy. A deep sleep fell upon me – a sleep like that of death. How long it lasted, of course, I know not; but when, once again, I unclosed my eyes, the objects around me were visible. By a wild sulfurous luster, the origin of which I could not at first determine, I was enabled to see the extent and aspect of the prison.

In its size I had been greatly mistaken. The whole circuit of its walls did not exceed twenty-five yards. For some minutes, this fact occasioned me a world of vain trouble; vain indeed! for what could be of less importance, under the terrible circumstances which environed me, than the mere dimensions of my dungeon? But my soul took a wild interest in trifles, and I busied myself in endeavors to account for the error I had committed in my measurement. The truth at length flashed upon me. In my first attempt at exploration I had counted fifty-two paces, up to the period when I fell; I must then have been within a pace or two of the fragment of serge; in fact I had nearly performed the circuit of the vault. I then slept, and upon awakening, I must have returned upon my steps – thus supposing the circuit nearly double what it actually was. My confusion of mind prevented me from observing that I began my tour with the wall to the left, and ended with the wall to my right.

I had been deceived, too, in respect of the shape of the enclosure. In feeling my way I had found many angles, and thus deduced an idea of great irregularity; so potent is the effect of total darkness upon one arousing from lethargy or sleep! The angles were simply those of a few slight depressions, or niches, at odd intervals. The general shape of the prison was square. What I had taken for masonry seemed now to be iron, or some other metal, in huge plates, whose sutures or joints occasioned the depression. The entire surface of this metallic enclosure was rudely daubed in all the hideous and repulsive devices to which the charnel superstition of the monks has given rise. The figures of fiends in aspects of menace, with skeleton forms, and other more really fearful images, overspread and disfigured the walls. I observed that the outlines of these monstrosities were sufficiently distinct, but that the colors seemed faded and blurred, as if from the effects of a damp atmosphere. I now noticed the floor, too, which was of stone. In the center yawned the circular pit from whose jaws I had escaped; but it was the only one in the dungeon.

All this I saw indistinctly and by much effort: for my personal condition had been greatly changed during slumber. I now lay upon my back, and at full length, on a species of low framework of wood. To this I was securely bound by a long strap resembling a surcingle. It passed in many convolutions about my limbs and body, leaving at liberty only my head, and my left arm to such extent that I could, by dint of much exertion, supply myself with food from an earthen dish which lay by my side on the floor. I saw, to my horror, that the pitcher had been removed. I say to my horror; for I was consumed with intolerable thirst. The thirst it appeared to be the design of my persecutors to stimulate: for the food in the dish was meat pungently spiced.

Looking upward, I surveyed the ceiling of my prison. It was some thirty or forty feet overhead, and constructed much as the side walls. In one of its panels, a very singular figure riveted my whole attention. It was the painted figure of Time as he is commonly represented, save that, in lieu of a scythe, he held what, at a casual glance, I supposed to be the pictured image of a huge pendulum such as we see on antique clocks. There was something, however, in the appearance of this machine which caused me to regard it more attentively. While I gazed directly upward at it (for its position was immediately over my own), I fancied that I saw it in motion. In an instant afterward, the fancy was confirmed. Its sweep was brief, and of course slow. I watched it for some minutes, somewhat in fear, but more in wonder. Wearied at length with observing its dull movement, I turned my eyes upon the other objects in the cell.

A slight noise attracted my notice, and, looking to the floor, I saw several enormous rats traversing it. They had issued from the well, which lay just within view to my right. Even then, while I gazed, they came up in troops, hurriedly, with ravenous eyes, allured by the scent of the meat. From this it required much effort and attention to scare them away.

It might have been half an hour, perhaps even an hour (for I could take but imperfect note of time), before I again cast my eyes upward. What I then saw confounded and amazed me. The sweep of the pendulum had increased in extent by nearly a yard. As a natural consequence, its velocity was also much greater. But what mainly disturbed me was the idea that it had perceptibly *descended*. I now observed – with what horror it is needless to say – that its nether extremity was formed of a crescent of glittering steel, about a foot in length from horn to horn; the horns upward, and the under edge evidently as keen as that of a razor. Like a razor also, it seemed massy and heavy, tapering from the edge into a solid and broad structure above. It was appended to a weighty rod of brass, and the whole *hissed* as it swung through the air.

I could no longer doubt the doom prepared for me by monkish ingenuity in torture. My cognizance of the pit had become known to the inquisitorial agents – *the pit* whose horrors had been destined for so bold a recusant as myself – *the pit*, typical of hell, and regarded by rumor as the Ultima Thule of all their punishments. The plunge into this pit I had avoided by the nearest of accidents, and I knew that surprise, or entrapment into torment, formed an important portion of all the grotesquerie of these dungeon deaths. Having failed to fall, it was no part of the demon plan to hurl me into the abyss; and thus (there being no alternative) a different and a milder destruction awaited me. Milder! I half smiled in my agony as I thought of such application of such a term.

What boots it to tell of the long, long hours of horror more than mortal, during which I counted the rushing vibrations of the steel! Inch by inch – line by line – with a descent only appreciable at intervals that seemed ages – down and still down it came! Days passed – it might have been that many days passed – ere it swept so closely over me as to fan me with its acrid breath. The odor of the sharp steel forced itself into my nostrils. I prayed – I wearied heaven with my prayer for its more speedy descent. I grew frantically mad, and struggled to force myself upward against the sweep of the fearful scimitar. And then I fell suddenly calm, and lay smiling at the glittering death, as a child at some rare bauble.

There was another interval of utter insensibility; it was brief; for, upon again lapsing into life there had been no perceptible descent in the pendulum. But it might have been long; for I knew there were demons who took note of my swoon, and who could have arrested the vibration at pleasure. Upon my recovery, too, I felt very – oh, inexpressibly sick and weak, as if through long inanition. Even amid the agonies of that period, the human nature craved food. With painful effort I outstretched my left arm as far as my bonds permitted and took possession of the small remnant which had been spared me by the rats. As I put a portion of it within my lips, there rushed to my mind a half-formed thought of joy – of hope. Yet what business had I with hope? It was, as I say, a half-formed thought – man has many such which are never completed. I felt that it was a joy – a hope; but I felt also that it had perished in its formation. In vain I struggled to perfect – to regain it. Long suffering had nearly annihilated all my ordinary powers of mind. I was an imbecile – an idiot.

The vibration of the pendulum was at right angles to my length. I saw that the crescent was designed to cross the region of the heart. It would fray the serge of my robe – it would return and repeat its operations – again – and again. Notwithstanding its terrifically wide sweep (some thirty feet or more) and the hissing vigor of its descent, sufficient to sunder these very walls of iron, still the fraying of my robe would be all that, for several minutes, it would accomplish. And at this thought I paused. I dared not go farther than this reflection. I dwelt upon it with a pertinacity of attention – as if, in so dwelling, I could arrest *here* the descent of steel. I forced myself to ponder upon the sound of the crescent as it should pass across the garment – upon the peculiar thrilling sensation which the friction of cloth produces on the nerves. I pondered upon all this frivolity until my teeth were on edge.

Down – steadily down it crept. I took a frenzied pleasure in contrasting its downward with its lateral velocity. To the right – to the left – far and wide – with the shriek of a damned spirit; to my heart with the stealthy pace of the tiger! I alternately laughed and howled as the one or the other idea grew predominant.

Down – certainly, relentlessly down! It vibrated within three inches of my bosom! I struggled violently, furiously, to free my left arm. This was free only from the elbow to the hand. I could reach the latter, from the platter beside me, to my mouth, with great effort, but no farther. Could I have broken the fastenings above the elbow, I would have seized and attempted to arrest the pendulum. I might as well have attempted to arrest an avalanche!

Down – still unceasingly – still inevitably down! I gasped and struggled at each vibration. I shrunk convulsively at its every sweep. My eyes followed its outward or upward whirls with the eagerness of the most unmeaning despair; they closed themselves spasmodically at the descent, although death would have been a relief. Oh! How unspeakable! Still I quivered in every nerve to think how slight a sinking of the machinery would precipitate that keen, glistening ax upon my bosom. It was *hope* that prompted the nerve to quiver – the frame to shrink. It was *hope* – the hope that triumphs on the rack – that whispers to the death-condemned even in the dungeons of the Inquisition.

I saw that some ten or twelve vibrations would bring the steel in actual contact with my robe, and with the observation there suddenly came over my spirit all the keen, collected calmness of despair. For the first time during many hours – or perhaps days – I *thought*. It now occurred to me that the bandage, or surcingle, which enveloped me, was *unique*. I was tied by no separate cord. The first stroke of the razor-like crescent athwart any portion of the band, would so detach it that it might be unwound from my person by means of my left hand. But how fearful, in that case, the proximity of the steel! The result of the slightest struggle how deadly! Was it likely, moreover, that the minions of the torturer had not foreseen and provided for this possibility! Was it probable that the bandage crossed my bosom in the track of the pendulum? Dreading to find my faint, and, as it seemed, my last hope frustrated, I so far elevated my head as to obtain a distinct view of my breast. The surcingle enveloped my limbs and body close in all directions – *save in the path of the destroying crescent.*

Scarcely had I dropped my head back into its original position, when there flashed upon my mind what I cannot better describe than as the unformed half of that idea of deliverance to which I have previously alluded, and of which a moiety only floated indeterminately through my brain when I raised food to my burning lips. The whole thought was now present – feeble, scarcely sane, scarcely definite, – but still entire. I proceeded at once, with the nervous energy of despair, to attempt its execution.

For many hours the immediate vicinity of the low framework upon which I lay had been literally swarming with rats. They were wild, bold, ravenous; their red eyes glaring upon me as if they waited but for motionlessness on my part to make me their prey. "To what food," I thought, "have they been accustomed in the well?"

They had devoured, in spite of all my efforts to prevent them, all but a small remnant of the contents of the dish. I had fallen into an habitual seesaw, or wave of the hand about the platter: and, at length, the unconscious uniformity of the movement deprived it of effect. In their voracity, the vermin frequently fastened their sharp fangs in my fingers. With the particles of the oily and spicy viand which now remained, I thoroughly rubbed the bandage wherever I could reach it; then, raising my hand from the floor, I lay breathlessly still.

At first, the ravenous animals were startled and terrified at the change – at the cessation of movement. They shrank alarmedly back; many sought the well. But this was only for a moment. I had not counted in vain upon their voracity. Observing that I remained without motion, one or two of the boldest leaped upon the framework and smelled at the surcingle. This seemed the signal for the general rush. Forth from the well they hurried in fresh troops. They clung to the wood – they overran it, and leaped in hundreds upon my person. The measured movement of the pendulum disturbed them not at all. Avoiding its strokes, they busied themselves with the anointed bandage. They pressed – they swarmed upon me in ever accumulating heaps. They writhed upon my throat; their cold lips sought my own; I was half stifled by their thronging pressure; disgust, for which the world has no name, swelled my bosom, and chilled, with a heavy clamminess, my heart. Yet one minute, and I felt that the struggle would be over. Plainly I perceived the loosening of the bandage. I knew that in more than one place it must be already severed. With a more than human resolution, I lay *still*.

Nor had I erred in my calculations – nor had I endured in vain. I at length felt that I was *free*. The surcingle hung in ribands from my body.

ALICE MEETS A DUCHESS

from
ALICE IN WONDERLAND
by
LEWIS CARROLL

Alice in Wonderland *is certainly one of the most famous stories ever written, for children or anybody else. It began as a tale told to three small English girls in a boat on the River Thames in 1862 by a mathematics lecturer at Oxford University, Charles Lutwidge Dodgson (Lewis Carroll was his pen-name). "Please write it down," cried one of the girls, Alice Liddell, when the boat trip was over; and that's what he did. It's an astonishing story of a dream that begins with Alice falling down a rabbit-hole, and progresses (backward and forward and even sideways) through one fantastic scene after another, with Alice now growing dangerously small, now dangerously large, and meeting some of the best-known characters in literature – the White Rabbit, the Queen of Hearts, the Ugly Duchess, the Cheshire Cat, the Mad Hatter, the March Hare...*

Lewis Carroll lived from 1832 to 1898. He wrote a second book about Alice's adventures, Through the Looking-Glass, *and a hair-raising nonsense poem,* The Hunting of the Snark.

F or a minute or two she stood looking at the house, and wondering what to do next, when suddenly a footman in livery came running out of the wood – (she considered him to be a footman because he was in livery: otherwise, judging by his face only, she would have called him a fish) – and rapped loudly at the door with his knuckles. It was opened by another footman in livery, with a round face, and large eyes like a frog; and both footmen, Alice noticed, had powdered hair that curled all over their heads. She felt very curious to know what it was all about, and crept a little way out of the wood to listen.

The Fish-Footman began by producing from under his arm a great letter, nearly as large as himself, and this he handed over to the other, saying, in a solemn tone, "For the Duchess. An invitation from the Queen to play croquet." The Frog-Footman repeated, in the same solemn tone, only changing the order of the words a little, "From the Queen. An invitation for the Duchess to play croquet."

Then they both bowed low, and their curls got entangled together.

Alice laughed so much at this, that she had to run back into the wood for fear of their hearing her; and when she next peeped out the Fish-Footman was gone, and the other was sitting on the ground near the door, staring stupidly up into the sky.

Alice went timidly up to the door and knocked.

"There's no sort of use in knocking," said the Footman,

"and that for two reasons. First, because I'm on the same side of the door as you are; second, because they're making such a noise inside, no one could possibly hear you." And certainly there was a most extraordinary noise going on within – a constant howling and sneezing, and every now and then a great crash, as if a dish or kettle had been broken to pieces.

"Please, then," said Alice, "how am I go get in?"

"There might be some sense in your knocking," the Footman went on without attending to her, "if we had the door between us. For instance, if you were *inside*, you might knock, and I could let you out, you know." He was looking up into the sky all the time he was speaking, and this Alice thought decidedly uncivil. "But perhaps he can't help it," she said to herself; "his eyes are so *very* nearly at the top of his head. But at any rate he might answer questions. – How am I to get in?" she repeated, aloud.

"I shall sit here," the Footman remarked, "till tomorrow –"

At this moment the door of the house opened, and a large plate came skimming out, straight at the Footman's head: it just grazed his nose, and broke to pieces against one of the trees behind him.

"– or next day, maybe," the Footman continued in the same tone, exactly as if nothing had happened.

"How am I to get in?" asked Alice again, in a louder tone.

"Are you to get in at all?" said the Footman. "That's the first question, you know."

It was, no doubt: only Alice did not like to be told so. "It's really dreadful," she muttered to herself, "the way all the creatures argue. It's enough to drive one crazy!"

The Footman seemed to think this a good opportunity for repeating his remark, with variations. "I shall sit here," he said, "on and off, for days and days."

"But what am *I* to do?" said Alice.

"Anything you like," said the Footman and began whistling.

"Oh, there's no use in talking to him," said Alice desperately: "he's perfectly idiotic!" And she opened the door and went in.

The door led right into a large kitchen, which was full of smoke from one end to the other: the Duchess was sitting on a three-legged stool in the middle, nursing a baby; the cook was leaning over the fire, stirring a large cauldron which seemed to be full of soup.

"There's certainly too much pepper in that soup!" Alice said to herself, as well as she could for sneezing.

There was certainly too much of it in the air. Even the Duchess sneezed occasionally; and as for the baby, it was sneezing and howling alternately without a moment's pause. The only things in the kitchen that did not sneeze were the cook and a large cat which was sitting on the hearth and grinning from ear to ear.

"Please would you tell me," said Alice, a little timidly, for she was not quite sure whether it was good manners for her to speak first, "why your cat grins like that?"

"It's a Cheshire cat," said the Duchess, "and that's why. Pig!"

She said the last word with such sudden violence that Alice quite jumped; but she saw in another moment that it was addressed to the baby, and not to her, so she took courage and went on again:–

"I didn't know that Cheshire cats always grinned; in fact, I didn't know that cats *could* grin."

"They all can," said the Duchess; "and most of 'em do."

"I don't know of any that do," Alice said very politely, feeling quite pleased to have got into a conversation.

"You don't know much," said the Duchess; "and that's a fact."

Alice did not at all like the tone of this remark, and thought it would be as well to introduce some other subject of conversation. While she was trying to fix on one, the cook took the cauldron of soup off the fire, and at once set to work throwing everything within her reach at the Duchess and the baby – the fire-irons came first; then followed a shower of saucepans, plates, and dishes. The Duchess took no notice of them even when they hit her; and the baby was howling so much already, that it was quite impossible to say whether the blows hurt it or not.

"Oh, *please* mind what you're doing!" cried Alice, jumping up and down in an agony of terror. "Oh, there goes his *precious* nose"; as an unusually large saucepan flew close by it and very nearly carried it off.

"If everybody minded their own business," the Duchess

said in a hoarse growl, "the world would go round a deal faster than it does."

"Which would *not* be an advantage," said Alice, who felt very glad to get an opportunity of showing off a little of her knowledge. "Just think of what work it would make with the day and night! You see the earth takes twenty-four hours to turn around on its axis –"

"Talking of axes," said the Duchess, "chop off her head!"

Alice glanced rather anxiously at the cook, to see if she meant to take the hint; but the cook was busily stirring the soup and seemed not to be listening, so she went on again: "Twenty-four hours, I *think*; or is it twelve? I –"

"Oh, don't bother *me*," said the Duchess; "I never could abide figures!" And with that she began nursing her child again, singing a sort of lullaby to it as she did so, and giving it a violent shake at the end of every line:

> *"Speak roughly to your little boy,*
> *And beat him when he sneezes:*
> *He only does it to annoy,*
> *Because he knows it teases."*

CHORUS
(In which the cook and the baby joined):–
"Wow! wow! wow!"

While the Duchess sang the second verse of the song, she kept tossing the baby violently up and down, and the poor little thing howled so, that Alice could hardly hear the words:–

> *"I speak severely to my boy.*
> *I beat him when he sneezes;*
> *For he can thoroughly enjoy*
> *The pepper when he pleases!"*

CHORUS
"Wow! wow! wow!"

"Here! you may nurse it a bit, if you like!" the Duchess said to Alice, flinging the baby at her as she spoke. "I must go and get ready to play croquet with the Queen," and she hurried out of the room. The cook threw a frying pan after her as she went out, but it just missed her.

Alice caught the baby with some difficulty, as it was a queer-shaped little creature, and held out its arms and legs in all directions, "just like a starfish," thought Alice. The poor little thing was snorting like a steam-engine when she caught it, and kept doubling itself up and straightening itself out again, so that altogether, for the first minute or two, it was as much as she could do to hold it.

As soon as she had made out the proper way of nursing it, (which was to twist it up into a sort of knot, and then keep hold of its right ear and left foot, so as to prevent its undoing itself,) she carried it out into the open air. "If I don't take this child away with me," thought Alice, "they're sure to kill it in a day or two: wouldn't it be murder to leave it behind?" She said the last words out loud, and the little thing grunted in reply (it had left off sneezing by this time). "Don't grunt," said Alice; "that's not at all a proper way of expressing yourself."

The baby grunted again, and Alice looked very anxiously into its face to see what was the matter with it. There could be no doubt that it had a *very* turn-up nose, much more like a snout than a real nose; also its eyes were getting extremely small for a baby: altogether Alice did not like the look of the thing at all. "But perhaps it was only sobbing," she thought, and looked into its eyes again, to see if there were any tears.

No, there were no tears. "If you're going to turn into a pig, my dear," said Alice, seriously, "I'll have nothing more to do with you. Mind now!" The poor little thing sobbed again (or grunted, it was impossible to say which), and they went on for some while in silence.

Alice was just beginning to think to herself, "Now, what am I to do with this creature when I get it home?" when it grunted again, so violently, that she looked down into its face in some alarm. This time there could be *no* mistake about it: it was neither more nor less than a pig, and she felt that it would be quite absurd for her to carry it any further.

So she set the little creature down and felt quite relieved to see it trot away quietly into the wood. "If it had grown up," she said to herself, "it would have made a dreadfully ugly child: but it makes rather a handsome pig, I think." And she began thinking over other children she knew who might do very well as pigs, and was just saying to herself, "if one only knew the right way to change them –" when she was a little startled by seeing the Cheshire Cat sitting on a bough of a tree a few yards off.

The Cat only grinned when it saw Alice. It looked good-natured, she thought: still, it had *very* long claws and a great many teeth, so she felt that it ought to be treated with respect.

"Cheshire Puss," she began, rather timidly, as she did not at all know whether it would like the name: however, it only grinned a little wider. "Come, it's pleased so far," thought Alice, and she went on. "Would you tell me, please, which way I ought to go from here?"

"That depends a good deal on where you want to get to," said the Cat.

"I don't much care where –" said Alice.

"Then it doesn't matter which way you go," said the Cat.

"– so long as I get *somewhere*," Alice added as an explanation.

"Oh, you're sure to do that," said the Cat, "if you only walk long enough."

Alice felt that this could not be denied, so she tried another question. "What sort of people live about here?"

"In *that* direction," the Cat said, waving its right paw round, "lives a Hatter: and in *that* direction," waving the other paw, "lives a March Hare. Visit either you like: they're both mad."

"But I don't want to go among mad people," Alice remarked.

"Oh, you can't help that," said the Cat: "we're all mad here. I'm mad. You're mad."

"How do you know I'm mad?" said Alice.

"You must be," said the Cat, "or you wouldn't have come here."

Alice didn't think that proved it at all; however, she went on "And how do you know that you're mad?"

"To begin with," said the Cat, "a dog's not mad. You grant that?"

"I suppose so," said Alice.

"Well, then," the Cat went on, "you see, a dog growls when it's angry, and wags its tail when it's pleased. Now *I* growl when I'm pleased, and wag my tail when I'm angry. Therefore I'm mad."

"I call it purring, not growling," said Alice.

"Call it what you like," said the Cat. "Do you play croquet with the Queen today?"

"I should like it very much," said Alice, "but I haven't been invited yet."

"You'll see me there," said the Cat, and vanished.

Alice was not much surprised at this, she was getting so used to queer things happening. While she was looking at the place where it had been, it suddenly appeared again.

"By-the-bye, what became of the baby?" said the Cat. "I'd nearly forgotten to ask."

"It turned into a pig," Alice quietly said, just as if it had come back in a natural way.

"I thought it would," said the Cat, and vanished again.

Alice waited a little, half expecting to see it again, but it did not appear, and after a minute or two, she walked on in the direction in which the March Hare was said to live. "I've seen hatters before," she said to herself; "the March Hare will be much the most interesting, and perhaps as this is May, it won't be raving mad – at least not so mad as it was in March." As she said this, she looked up, and there was the Cat again, sitting on a branch of a tree.

"Did you say pig, or fig?" said the Cat.

"I said pig," replied Alice; "and I wish you wouldn't keep appearing and vanishing so suddenly: you make one quite giddy."

"All right," said the Cat; and this time it vanished quite slowly, beginning with the end of the tail, and ending with the grin, which remained some time after the rest of it had gone.

"Well! I've often seen a cat without a grin," thought Alice; "but a grin without a cat! It's the most curious thing I ever saw in all my life!"

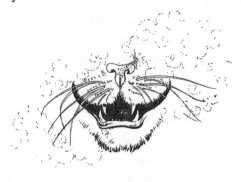

JIM FIGHTS ISRAEL HANDS

from
TREASURE ISLAND
by
R. L. STEVENSON

Stevenson, who lived from 1850 to 1895, was the son of a builder of lighthouses, and he angered his father by wanting to write rather than be an engineer. He wrote Treasure Island *for his stepson in enormous, excited haste in 1881: in a letter to a friend, he said that "it begins in the 'Admiral Benbow' public house on the Devon coast... It's all about a map, and a treasure, and a mutiny, and a derelict ship, and a current, and a fine old Squire Trelawney, and a doctor, and a sea-cook with one leg, and a sea-song with the chorus 'Yo-ho-ho and a bottle of rum' (at the third Ho you heave at the capstan bars) which is a real buccaneer's song,*

only known to the crew of the late Captain Flint..." And no more need be said: except that the crew of the treasure ship Hispaniola *are led into mutiny by Long John Silver, the one-legged cook; and at a desperate moment after they've reached the island, Jim Hawkins finds the* Hispaniola *adrift. Of the two watchmen left aboard by the mutineers, one lies dead, killed in a drunken brawl by the other, the coxswain Israel Hands. Badly wounded, Hands promises to help Jim sail the ship to a safe anchorage.*

Much more of Stevenson awaits those who haven't read him – especially Kidnapped, *an intensely exciting story set in the Highlands of Scotland after the 1745 rebellion, and, for those who enjoy or positively welcome horrific stories,* Dr. Jekyll and Mr. Hyde.

T he wind, serving us to a desire, now hauled into the west. We could run so much the easier from the northeast corner of the island to the mouth of the North Inlet. Only, as we had no power to anchor, and dared not beach her till the tide had flowed a good deal farther, time hung on our hands. The coxswain told me how to lay the ship to; after a good many trials I succeeded, and we both sat in silence, over another meal.

"Cap'n," said he, at length, with that same uncomfortable smile, "here's my old shipmate, O'Brien; s'pose you was to heave him overboard. I ain't partic'lar as a rule, and I don't take no blame for settling his hash; but I don't reckon him ornamental, now, do you?"

"I'm not strong enough, and I don't like the job; and there he lies, for me," said I.

"This here's an unlucky ship – this *Hispaniola*, Jim," he

went on, blinking. "There's a power of men been killed in this *Hispaniola* – a sight o' poor seamen dead and gone since you and me took ship to Bristol. I never seen sich dirty luck, not I. There was this here O'Brien, now – he's dead, ain't he? Well, now, I'm no scholar, and you're a lad as can read and figure; and to put it straight, do you take it as a dead man is dead for good, or do he come alive again?"

"You can kill the body, Mr. Hands, but not the spirit; you must know that already," I replied. "O'Brien there is in another world, and maybe watching us."

"Ah!" says he. "Well, that's unfort'nate – appears as if killing parties was a waste of time. Howsomever, sperrits don't reckon for much, by what I've seen. I'll chance it with the sperrits, Jim. And now, you've spoke up free, and I'll take it kind if you'd step down into that there cabin and get me a – well, a – shiver my timbers! I can't hit the name on't; well, you get me a bottle of wine, Jim – this here brandy's too strong for my head."

Now, the coxswain's hesitation seemed to be unnatural; and as for the notion of his preferring wine to brandy, I entirely disbelieved it. The whole story was a pretext. He wanted me to leave the deck – so much was plain; but with what purpose I could in no way imagine. His eyes never met mine; they kept wandering to and fro, up and down, now with a look to the sky, now with a flitting glance upon the dead O'Brien. All the time he kept smiling, and putting his tongue out in the most guilty, embarrassed manner, so that a child could have told that he was bent on some deception. I was prompt with my answer, however, for I saw where my advantage lay; and that with a fellow so densely stupid I could easily conceal my suspicions to the end.

"Some wine?" I said. "Far better. Will you have white or red?"

"Well, I reckon it's about the blessed same to me, shipmate," he replied; "so it's strong, and plenty of it, what's the odds?"

"All right," I answered. "I'll bring you port, Mr. Hands. But I'll have to dig for it."

With that, I scuttled down the companion with all the noise I could, slipped off my shoes, ran quietly along the sparred gallery, mounted the forecastle ladder, and popped my head out of the fore companion. I knew he would not expect to see me there; yet I took every precaution possible; and certainly the worst of my suspicions proved too true.

He had risen from his position to his hands and knees; and, though his leg obviously hurt him pretty sharply when he moved – for I could hear him stifle a groan – yet it was at a good, rattling rate that he trailed himself across the deck. In half a minute, he had reached the port scuppers and picked out of a coil of rope, a long knife, or rather a short dirk, discolored to the hilt with blood. He looked upon it for a moment, thrusting forth his under jaw, tried the point upon his hand, and then, hastily concealing it in the bosom of his jacket, trundled back again into his old place against the bulwark.

This was all that I required to know. Israel could move

about; he was now armed; and if he had been at so much trouble to get rid of me, it was plain that I was meant to be the victim. What he would do afterward – whether he would try to crawl right across the island from North Inlet to the camp among the swamps, or whether he would fire Long Tom, trusting that his own comrades might come first to help him, was, of course, more than I could say.

Yet I felt sure that I could trust him in one point, since in that our interests jumped together, and that was in the disposition of the schooner. We both desired to have her stranded safe enough, in a sheltered place, and so that, when the time came, she could be got off again with as little labor and danger as might be; and until that was done, I considered that my life would certainly be spared.

While I was thus turning the business over in my mind, I had not been with my body. I had stolen back to the cabin, slipped once more into my shoes, and laid my hand at random on a bottle of wine, and now, with this for an excuse, I made my reappearance on the deck.

Hands lay as I had left him, all fallen together in a bundle, and with his eyelids lowered, as though he were too weak to bear the light. He looked up, however, at my coming, knocked the neck of the bottle, like a man who had done the same thing often, and took a good swig, with his favorite toast of "Here's luck!" Then he lay quiet for a little, and then, pulling out a stick of tobacco, begged me to cut him a quid.

"Cut me a junk o' that," says he, "for I haven't no knife,

and hardly strength enough, so be as I had. Ah, Jim, Jim, I reckon I've missed stays! Cut me a quid, as 'll likely be the last, lad; for I'm for my long home, and no mistake."

"Well," said I, "I'll cut you some tobacco; but if I was you and thought myself so badly, I would go to my prayers, like a Christian man."

"Why?" said he. "Now, you tell me why."

"Why?" I cried. "You were asking me just now about the dead. You've broken your trust; you've lived in sin and lies and blood; there's a man you killed lying at your feet this moment; and you ask me why! For God's mercy, Mr. Hands, that's why."

I spoke with a little heat, thinking of the bloody dirk he had hidden in his pocket, and designed, in his ill thoughts, to end me with. He, for his part, took a great draft of the wine and spoke with the most unusual solemnity.

"For thirty years," he said, "I've sailed the seas and seen good and bad, better and worse, fair weather and foul, provisions running out, knives going, and what not. Well, now I tell you, I never seen good come o' goodness yet. Him as strikes first is my fancy; dead men don't bite; them's my views – amen, so be it. And now, you look here," he added, suddenly changing his tone, "we've had about enough of this foolery. The tide's made good enough by now. You just take my orders, Cap'n Hawkins, and we'll sail slap in and be done with it."

All told, we had scarce two miles to run; but the navigation was delicate, the entrance to this northern anchorage was not only narrow and shoal, but lay east and west, so that the schooner must be nicely handled to be got in. I think I was a very good, prompt subaltern, and I am very sure that Hands was an excellent pilot; for we went about and about, and dodged in, shaving the banks, with a certainty and a neatness that were a pleasure to behold.

Scarcely had we passed the heads before the land closed around us. The shores of North Inlet were as thickly wooded as those of the southern anchorage; but the space was longer and narrower, and more like what in truth it was, the estuary of a river. Right before us, at the southern end, we saw the wreck of a ship in the last stages of dilapidation. It had been a great vessel of three masts, but had lain so long exposed to the injuries of the weather that it was hung about with great webs of dripping seaweed, and on the deck of it shore bushes had taken root and now flourished thick with flowers. It was a sad sight, but it showed us that the anchorage was calm.

"Now," said Hands, "look there; there's a pet bit to beach a ship in. Fine flat sand, never a catspaw, trees all around of it, and flowers a-blowing like a garding on that old ship."

"And once beached," I enquired, "how shall we get her off again?"

"Why, so," he replied; "you take a line ashore there on the other side at low water: take a turn about one o' them big pines; bring it back, take a turn around the capstan, and lie-to for the tide. Come high water, all hands take a pull upon the line, and off she comes as sweet as natur'. And now, boy, you stand by. We're near the bit now, and she's too much way on her. Starboard a little – so – steady – starboard – larboard a little – steady – steady!"

So he issued his commands, while I breathlessly obeyed; till, all of a sudden, he cried, "Now, my hearty, luff!" And I put the helm hard up, and the *Hispaniola* swung around rapidly and ran stem on for the low wooded shore.

The excitement of these last maneuvers had somewhat interfered with the watch I had kept hitherto, sharply enough, upon the coxswain. Even then, I was still so much interested, waiting for the ship to touch, that I had quite forgot the peril that hung over my head and stood craning over the starboard bulwarks and watching the ripples spreading wide before the bows. I might have fallen without a struggle for my life, had not a sudden disquietude seized upon me and made me turn my head. Perhaps I had heard a creak, or seen his shadow moving with the tail of my eye; perhaps it was an instinct like a cat's; but, sure enough, when I looked around, there was Hands, already halfway toward me, with the dirk in his right hand.

We must both have cried out aloud when our eyes met; but while mine was the shrill cry of terror, his was a roar of fury like a charging bull's. At the same instant, he threw himself forward, and I leapt sideways toward the bows. As I did so, I left hold of the tiller, which sprang sharp to leeward; and I think this saved my life, for it struck Hands across the chest and stopped him, for the moment, dead.

Before he could recover, I was safe out of the corner

where he had me trapped, with all the deck to dodge about. Just forward of the mainmast, I stopped, drew a pistol from my pocket, took a cool aim, though he had already turned and was once more coming directly after me, and drew the trigger. The hammer fell, but there followed neither flash nor sound; the priming was useless with sea water. I cursed myself for my neglect. Why had not I, long before, reprimed and reloaded my only weapons? Then I should not have been, as now, a mere fleeing sheep before this butcher.

Wounded as he was, it was wonderful how fast he could move, his grizzled hair tumbling over his face, and his face itself as red as a red ensign with his haste and fury. I had no time to try my other pistol, nor, indeed, much inclination, for I was sure it would be useless. One thing I saw plainly: I must not simply retreat before him, or he would speedily hold me boxed into the bows, as a moment since he had so nearly boxed me in the stern. Once so caught, and nine or ten inches of the blood-stained dirk would be my last experience on this side of eternity. I placed my palms against the mainmast, which was of a goodish bigness, and waited, every nerve upon the stretch.

Seeing that I meant to dodge, he also paused; and a moment or two passed in feints on his part, and corresponding movements upon mine. It was such a game as I had often played at home about the rocks of Black Hill Cove; but never before, you may be sure, with such a wildly beating heart as now. Still, as I say, it was a boy's game, and I thought I could hold my own at it, against an elderly seaman with a wounded thigh. Indeed, my courage had begun to rise so high, that I allowed myself a few darting thoughts on what would be the end of the affair; and while I saw certainly that I could spin it out for long, I saw no hope of any ultimate escape.

Well, while things stood thus, suddenly the *Hispaniola* struck, staggered, ground for an instant in the sand, and then, swift as a blow, canted over to the port side, till the deck stood at an angle of forty-five degrees, and about a puncheon of water splashed into the scupper-holes, and lay, in a pool, between the deck and bulwark.

We were both of us capsized in a second, and both of us rolled, almost together, into the scuppers; the dead red-cap, with his arms still spread out, tumbling stiffly after us. So near were we, indeed, that my head came against the coxswain's foot with a crack that made my teeth rattle. Blow and all, I was the first afoot again; for Hands had got involved with the dead body. The sudden canting of the ship had made the deck no place for running on; I had to find some new way of escape, and that upon the instant, for my foe was almost touching me. Quick as thought, I sprang into the mizzen shrouds, rattled up hand over hand, and did not draw a breath till I was seated on the cross-trees.

I had been saved by being prompt; the dirk had struck not half a foot below me, as I pursued my upward flight; and there stood Israel Hands with his mouth open and his face upturned to mine, a perfect statue of surprise and disappointment.

Now that I had a moment to myself, I lost no time in changing the priming of my pistol, and then, having one ready for service, and to make assurance doubly sure, I proceeded to draw the load of the other and recharge it afresh from the beginning.

My new employment struck Hands all of a heap; he began to see the dice going against him; and after an obvious hesitation, he also hauled himself heavily into the shrouds, and, with the dirk in his teeth, began slowly and painfully to mount. It cost him no end of time and groans to haul his wounded leg behind him; and I had quietly finished my arrangements before he was much more than a third of the way up. Then, with a pistol in either hand, I addressed him.

"One more step, Mr. Hands," said I, "and I'll blow your brains out! Dead men don't bite, you know," I added, with a chuckle.

He stopped instantly. I could see by the working of his face that he was trying to think, and the process was so slow and laborious that, in my new-found security, I laughed aloud. At last, with a swallow or two, he spoke, his face still wearing the same expression of extreme perplexity. In order to speak, he had to take the dagger from his mouth, but, in all else, he remained unmoved.

"Jim," says he, "I reckon we're fouled, you and me, and we'll have to sign articles. I'd have had you but for that there lurch; but I don't have no luck, not I; and I reckon I'll have to strike, which comes hard, you see, for a master mariner to a ship's younker like you, Jim."

I was drinking in his words and smiling away, as conceited as a cock upon a wall, when, all in a breath, back went his right hand over his shoulder. Something sang like an arrow through the air; I felt a blow and then a sharp pang, and there I was pinned by the shoulder to the mast. In the horrid pain and surprise of the moment – I scarce can say it was by my own volition, and I am sure it was without a conscious aim – both my pistols went off, and both escaped out of my hands. They did not fall alone; with a choked cry, the coxswain loosed his grasp upon the shrouds and plunged head first into the water.

WILBUR'S ESCAPE

from
CHARLOTTE'S WEB
by
E. B. WHITE

Charlotte's Web *first published in 1952, is about as close to perfect as a children's story ever was. The scene is a farm, and the principal characters are: Wilbur, a very young pig who enjoys his food, the fond attention of a little girl called Fern, and the lively society of farmyard and barn, but does not enjoy the discovery that he is being fattened up as part of Mr. Zuckerman's proposed Christmas dinner; and Charlotte, a spider, who launches a campaign involving some astonishing feats of web-making, to (literally) save Wilbur's bacon. In the passage that follows, Wilbur has only just arrived at Mr. Zuckerman's farm.*

E. B. White (who lived from 1899 to 1985) also wrote Stuart Little, *the story of a distinctly unusual mouse.*

T he barn was very large. It was very old. It smelled of hay, and it smelled of manure. It smelled of the perspiration of tired horses and the wonderful sweet breath of patient cows. It often had a peaceful sort of smell – as though nothing bad could ever happen again in the world. It smelled of grain and of harness dressing and of axle grease and of rubber boots and of new rope. And whenever the cat was given a fish-head to eat, the barn would smell of fish. But mostly it smelled of hay, for there was always hay being pitched down to the cows and the horses and the sheep.

The barn was pleasantly warm in winter when the animals spent most of their time indoors, and it was pleasantly cool in summer when the big doors stood wide open to the breeze. The barn had stalls on the main floor for the work horses, tie-ups on the main floor for the cows, a sheepfold down below for the sheep, a pigpen down below for Wilbur, and it was full of all sorts of things that you find in barns: ladders, grindstones, pitchforks, monkey wrenches, scythes, lawn mowers, snow shovels, ax handles, milk pails, water buckets, empty grain sacks, and rusty rat traps. It was the kind of barn that swallows like to build their nests in. It was the kind of barn that children like to play in. And the whole thing was owned by Fern's uncle, Mr. Homer L. Zuckerman.

Wilbur's new home was in the lower part of the barn, directly underneath the cows. Mr. Zuckerman knew that a manure pile is a good place to keep a young pig. Pigs need warmth, and it was warm and comfortable down there in the barn cellar on the south side.

Fern came, almost every day, to visit him. She found an old milking stool that had been discarded, and she placed the stool in the sheepfold next to Wilbur's pen. Here she sat quietly during the long afternoons, thinking and listening and watching Wilbur. The sheep soon got to know her and trust her. So did the geese, who lived with the sheep. All the animals trusted her, she was so quiet and friendly. Mr. Zuckerman did not allow her to take Wilbur out, and he did not allow her to get into the pigpen. But he told Fern that she could sit on the stool and watch Wilbur as long as she wanted to. It made her happy just to be near the pig, and it made Wilbur happy to know that she was sitting there, right outside his pen. But he never had any fun – no walks, no rides, no swims.

One afternoon in June, when Wilbur was almost two months old, he wandered out into his small yard outside the barn. Fern had not arrived for her usual visit. Wilbur stood in the sun feeling lonely and bored.

"There's never anything to do around here," he thought. He walked slowly to his food trough and sniffed to see if anything had been overlooked at lunch. He found a small strip of potato skin and ate it. His back itched, so he leaned against the fence and rubbed against the boards. When he tired of this, he walked indoors, climbed to the top of the manure pile, and sat down. He didn't feel like going to sleep, he didn't feel like digging, he was tired of standing still, tired of lying down. "I'm less than two months old, and I'm tired of living," he said. He walked out to the yard again.

"When I'm out here," he said, "there's no place to go but in. When I'm indoors, there's no place to go but back out in the yard."

"That's where you're wrong, my friend, my friend," said a voice.

Wilbur looked through the fence and saw the goose standing there.

"You don't have to stay in that dirty-little dirty-little dirty-little yard," said the goose, who talked rather fast. "One of the boards is loose. Push on it, push-push-push on it, and come on out!"

"What?" said Wilbur. "Say it slower!"

"At-at-at, at the risk of repeating myself," said the goose, "I suggest that you come on out. It's wonderful out here."

"Did you say a board was loose?"

"That I did, that I did," said the goose.

Wilbur walked up to the fence and saw that the goose was right – one board was loose. He put his head down, shut his eyes, and pushed. The board gave way. In a minute, he had squeezed through the fence and was standing in the long grass outside his yard. The goose chuckled.

"How does it feel to be free?" she asked.

"I like it," said Wilbur. "That is, I *guess* I like it." Actually, Wilbur felt queer to be outside his fence, with nothing between him and the big world.

"Where do you think I'd better go?"

"Anywhere you like, anywhere you like," said the goose.

"Go down through the orchard, root up the sod! Go down through the garden, dig up the radishes! Root up everything! Eat grass! Look for corn! Look for oats! Run all over! Skip and dance, jump and prance! Go down through the orchard and stroll in the woods! The world is a wonderful place when you're young."

"I can see that," replied Wilbur. He gave a jump in the air, twirled, ran a few steps, stopped, looked all around, sniffed the smells of afternoon, and then set off walking down through the orchard. Pausing in the shade of an apple tree, he put his strong snout into the ground and began pushing, digging, and rooting. He felt very happy. He had plowed up quite a piece of ground before anyone noticed him. Mrs. Zuckerman was the first to see him. She saw him from the kitchen window, and she immediately shouted for the men.

"Ho-*mer*!" she cried. "Pig's out! Lurvy! Pig's out! Homer! Lurvy! Pig's out. He's down there under that apple tree."

"Now the trouble starts," thought Wilbur. "Now I'll catch it."

The goose heard the racket and she, too, started hollering. "Run-run-run downhill, make for the woods, the woods!" she shouted to Wilbur. "They'll never-never-never catch you in the woods."

The cocker spaniel heard the commotion, and he ran out from the barn to join in the chase. Mr. Zuckerman heard, and he came out of the machine shed where he was mending a tool. Lurvy, the hired man, heard the noise and came up from the asparagus patch where he was pulling weeds.

Everybody walked toward Wilbur, and Wilbur didn't know what to do. The woods seemed a long way off, and anyway, he had never been down there in the woods and wasn't sure he would like it.

"Get around behind him, Lurvy," said Mr. Zuckerman, "and drive him toward the barn! And take it easy – don't rush him! I'll go and get a bucket of slops."

The news of Wilbur's escape spread rapidly among the animals on the place. Whenever any creature broke loose on Zuckerman's farm, the event was of great interest to the others. The goose shouted to the nearest cow that Wilbur was free, and soon all the cows knew. Then one of the cows told one of the sheep, and soon all the sheep knew. The lambs learned about it from their mothers. The horses, in their stalls in the barn, pricked up their ears when they heard the goose hollering; and soon the horses had caught on to what was happening. "Wilbur's out," they said. Every animal stirred its head and became excited to know that one of its friends had got free and was no longer penned up or tied fast.

Wilbur didn't know what to do or which way to run. It seemed as though everybody was after him. "If this is what it's like to be free," he thought, "I believe I'd rather be penned up in my own yard."

The cocker spaniel was sneaking up on him from one side, Lurvy the hired man was sneaking up on him from the other side. Mrs. Zuckerman stood ready to head him off if he started for the garden, and now Mr. Zuckerman was coming down toward him carrying a pail. "This is really awful," thought Wilbur. "Why doesn't Fern come?" He began to cry.

The goose took command and began to give orders.

"Don't just stand there, Wilbur! Dodge about, dodge about!" cried the goose. "Skip around, run toward me, slip in and out, in and out, in and out! Make for the woods! Twist and turn!"

The cocker spaniel sprang for Wilbur's hind leg. Wilbur jumped and ran. Lurvy reached out and grabbed. Mrs. Zuckerman screamed at Lurvy. The goose cheered for Wilbur. Wilbur dodged between Lurvy's legs. Lurvy missed Wilbur and grabbed the spaniel instead. "Nicely done, nicely done!" cried the goose. "Try it again, try it again."

"Run downhill!" suggested the cows.

"Run toward me!" yelled the gander.

"Run uphill!" cried the sheep.

"Turn and twist!" honked the goose.

"Jump and dance!" said the rooster.

"Look out for Lurvy!" called the cows.

"Look out for Zuckerman!" yelled the gander.

"Watch out for the dog!" cried the sheep.

"Listen to me, listen to me!" screamed the goose.

Poor Wilbur was dazed and frightened by this hullabaloo. He didn't like being the center of all this fuss. He tried to follow the instructions his friends were giving him, but he couldn't run downhill and uphill at the same time, and he couldn't turn and twist when he was jumping and dancing, and he was crying so hard he could barely see anything that was happening. After all, Wilbur was a very young pig – not much more than a baby, really. He wished Fern were here to take him in her arms and comfort him. When he looked up and saw Mr. Zuckerman standing quite close to him, holding a pail of warm slops, he felt relieved. He lifted his nose and sniffed. The smell was delicious – warm milk, potato skins, wheat middlings, Toasted Corn Flakes, and a popover left from the Zuckermans' breakfast.

"Come, pig!" said Mr. Zuckerman, tapping the pail. "Come, pig!"

Wilbur took a step toward the pail.

"No-no-no!" said the goose. "It's the old pail trick, Wilbur. Don't fall for it, don't fall for it! He's trying to lure you back into captivity-ivity. He's appealing to your stomach."

Wilbur didn't care. The food smelled appetizing. He took another step toward the pail.

"Pig, pig!" said Mr. Zuckerman in a kind voice, and began walking slowly toward the barnyard, looking all about him innocently, as if he didn't know that a little white pig was following along behind him.

"You'll be sorry-sorry-sorry," called the goose.

Wilbur didn't care. He kept walking toward the pail of slops.

"You'll miss your freedom," honked the goose. "An hour of freedom is worth a barrel of slops."

Wilbur didn't care.

When Mr. Zuckerman reached the pigpen, he climbed over the fence and poured the slops into the trough. Then he pulled the loose board away from the fence, so that there was a wide hole for Wilbur to walk through.

"Reconsider, reconsider!" cried the goose.

Wilbur paid no attention. He stepped through the fence into his yard. He walked to the trough and took a long drink of slops, sucking in the milk hungrily and chewing the popover. It was good to be home again.

While Wilbur ate, Lurvy fetched a hammer and some eight-penny nails and nailed the board in place. Then he and Mr. Zuckerman leaned lazily on the fence, and Mr. Zuckerman scratched Wilbur's back with a stick.

"He's quite a pig," said Lurvy.

"Yes, he'll make a good pig," said Mr. Zuckerman.

Wilbur heard the words of praise. He felt the warm milk inside his stomach. He felt the pleasant rubbing of the stick along his itchy back. He felt peaceful and happy and sleepy. This had been a tiring afternoon. It was still only about four o' clock, but Wilbur was ready for bed.

"I'm really too young to go out into the world alone," he thought as he lay down.

THE WAGER

from
THE CALL OF THE WILD
by
JACK LONDON

Jack London was always astonished by the marvel of life, and of human strength, and by the often desperate nature of our struggle to stay alive. In The Call of the Wild *(and in another novel,* White Fang*), he expressed these feelings of his in stories about animals. Buck, a dog (his father was a St. Bernard, his mother a Scottish sheepdog), is stolen from his owner on a comfortable estate in California, and sold in Alaska – this being the time of the great goldrush, when dogs were immensely valuable. Buck passes from bad owners to good ones, faces death a score of times, and in the end escapes to the wild life that has always been calling to him. In the passage below, he is in the hands of a good master, John Thornton, and Thornton's partners, Hans and Pete. Buck leads their team of dogs.*

Jack London lived from 1876 to 1919.

T hat winter, at Dawson, Buck performed another exploit, not so heroic, perhaps, but one that put his name many notches higher on the totem pole of Alaskan fame. This exploit was particularly gratifying to the three men; for they stood in need of the outfit which it furnished and were enabled to make a long-desired trip into the virgin East, where miners had not yet appeared. It was brought about by a conversation in the Eldorado Saloon, in which men waxed boastful of their favorite dogs. Buck, because of his record, was the target for these men, and Thornton was driven stoutly to defend him. At the end of half an hour, one man stated that his dog could start a sled with five hundred pounds and walk off with it; a second bragged six hundred for his dog; and a third seven hundred.

"Pooh! pooh!" said John Thornton. "Buck can start a thousand pounds."

"And break it out? and walk off with it for a hundred yards?" demanded Matthewson, a Bonanza King, he of the seven hundred vaunt.

"And break it out, and walk off with it for a hundred yards," John Thornton said coolly.

"Well," Matthewson said slowly and deliberately, so that all could hear, "I've got a thousand dollars that he says he can't. And there it is." So saying, he slammed a sack of gold dust of the size of a bologna sausage down upon the bar.

Nobody spoke. Thornton's bluff, if bluff it was, had been called. He could feel a flush of warm blood creeping up his face. His tongue had tricked him. He did not know whether Buck could start a thousand pounds. Half a ton! The enormousness of it appalled him. He had great faith in Buck's strength and had often thought him capable of starting such a load; but never, as now, had he faced the possibility of it, the eyes of a dozen men fixed upon him, silent and waiting. Further, he had no thousand dollars; nor had Hans or Pete.

"I've got a sled standing outside now, with twenty fifty-pound sacks of flour on it," Matthewson went on with brutal directness, "so don't let that hinder you."

Thornton did not reply. He did not know what to say. He glanced from face to face in the absent way of a man who has lost the power of thought and is seeking somewhere to find the thing that will start it going again. The face of Jim O'Brien, a Mastodon King and old-time comrade, caught his eyes. It was as a cue to him, seeming to rouse him to do what he would never have dreamed of doing.

"Can you lend me a thousand?" he asked, almost in a whisper.

"Sure," answered O'Brien, thumping down a plethoric sack by the side of Matthewson's. "Though it's little faith I'm having, John, that the beast can do the trick."

The Eldorado emptied its occupants into the street to see the test. The tables were deserted, and the dealers and gamekeepers came forth to see the outcome of the wager and to lay odds. Several hundred men, furred and mittened, banked around the sled within easy distance. Matthewson's sled, loaded with a thousand pounds of flour, had been standing for a couple of hours, and in the intense cold (it was sixty below zero) the runners had frozen fast to the hard-packed snow. Men offered odds of two to one that Buck could not budge the sled. A quibble arose concerning the phrase "break out." O'Brien contended it was Thornton's privilege to knock the runners loose, leaving Buck to "break it out" from a dead standstill. Matthewson insisted that the phrase included breaking the runners from the frozen grip of the snow. A majority of the men who had witnessed the making of the bet decided in his favor, whereat the odds went up to three to one against Buck.

There were no takers. Not a man believed him capable of the feat. Thornton had been hurried into the wager, heavy with doubt; and now that he looked at the sled itself, the concrete fact, with the regular team of ten dogs curled up in the snow before it, the more impossible the task appeared. Matthewson waxed jubilant.

"Three to one!" he proclaimed. "I'll lay you another thousand at that figure, Thornton. What d'ye say?"

Thornton's doubt was strong in his face, but his fighting spirit was aroused – the fighting spirit that soars above the odds, fails to recognize the impossible, and is deaf to all save the clamor for battle. He called Hans and Pete to him. Their sacks were slim, and with his own, the three partners could rake together only two hundred dollars. In the ebb of their fortunes, this sum was their total capital; yet they laid it unhesitatingly against Matthewson's six hundred.

The team of ten dogs was unhitched, and Buck, with his own harness, was put into the sled. He had caught the contagion of the excitement, and he felt that in some way he must do a great thing for John Thornton. Murmurs of admiration at his splendid appearance went up. He was in perfect condition, without an ounce of superfluous flesh, and the one hundred and fifty pounds that he weighed were so many pounds of grit and virility. His furry coat shone with the sheen of silk. Down the neck and across the shoulders, his mane, in repose as it was, half bristled and seemed to lift with every movement, as though excess of vigor made each particular hair alive and active. The great breast and heavy forelegs were no more than in proportion with the rest of the body, where the muscles showed in tight rolls underneath the skin. Men felt these muscles and proclaimed them hard as iron, and the odds went down to two to one.

"Gad, sir! Gad sir!" stuttered a member of the latest dynasty, a king of the Skookum Benches. "I offer you eight hundred for him, sir, before the test, sir; eight hundred just as he stands."

Thornton shook his head and stepped to Buck's side.

"You must stand off from him," Matthewson protested. "Free play and plenty of room."

The crowd fell silent; only could be heard the voices of the gamblers vainly offering two to one. Everybody acknowledged Buck a magnificent animal, but twenty fifty-pound sacks of flour bulked too large in their eyes for them to loosen their pouch-strings.

Thornton knelt down by Buck's side. He took his head in his two hands and rested cheek on cheek. He did not playfully shake him, as was his wont, or murmur soft love curses; but he whispered in his ear. "As you love me, Buck. As you love me," was what he whispered. Buck whined with suppressed eagerness.

The crowd was watching curiously. The affair was growing mysterious. It seemed like a conjuration. As Thornton got to his feet, Buck seized his mittened hand between his jaws, pressing in with his teeth and releasing slowly, half-reluctantly. It was the answer, in terms, not of speech, but of love. Thornton stepped well back.

"Now, Buck," he said.

Buck tightened the traces, then slacked them for a matter of several inches. It was the way he had learned.

"Gee!" Thornton's voice rang out, sharp in the tense silence.

Buck swung to the right, ending the movement in a plunge that took up the slack and with a sudden jerk arrested his one hundred and fifty pounds. The load quivered, and from under the runners arose a crisp crackling.

"Haw!" Thornton commanded.

Buck duplicated the maneuver, this time to the left. The crackling turned into a snapping, the sled pivoting and the runners slipping and grating several inches to the side. The sled was broken out. Men were holding their breaths, intensely unconscious of the fact.

"Now, MUSH!"

Thornton's command cracked out like a pistol shot. Buck threw himself forward, tightening the traces with a jarring lunge. His whole body was gathered compactly together in the tremendous effort, the muscles writhing and knotting like live things under the silky fur. His great chest was low to the ground, his head forward and down, while his feet were flying like mad, the claws scarring the hard-packed snow in parallel grooves. The sled swayed and trembled, half-started forward. One of his feet slipped, and one man groaned aloud. Then the sled lurched ahead in what appeared a rapid succession of jerks, though it never really came to a dead stop again... half an inch... an inch... two inches... The jerks perceptibly diminished; as the sled gained momentum, he caught them up, till it was moving steadily along.

Men gasped and began to breathe again, unaware that for a moment they had ceased to breathe. Thornton was running behind, encouraging Buck with short, cheery words. The distance had been measured off, and as he neared the pile of firewood which marked the end of the hundred yards, a cheer began to grow and grow, which burst into a roar as he passed the firewood and halted at command. Every man was tearing himself loose, even Matthewson. Hats and mittens were flying in the air. Men were shaking hands, it did not matter with whom, and bubbling over in a general incoherent babel.

But Thornton fell on his knees beside Buck. Head was against head, and he was shaking him back and forth. Those who hurried up heard him cursing Buck, and he cursed him long and fervently, and softly and lovingly.

"Gad, sir! Gad sir!" spluttered the Skookum Bench king. "I'll give you a thousand for him, sir, a thousand, sir – twelve hundred, sir."

Thornton rose to his feet. His eyes were wet. The tears were streaming frankly down his cheeks. "Sir," he said to the Skookum Bench king, "no, sir. You can go to hell, sir. It's the best I can do for you, sir."

Buck seized Thornton's hand in his teeth. Thornton shook him back and forth. As though animated by a common impulse, the onlookers drew back to a respectful distance; nor were they again indiscreet enough to interrupt.

UP THE ZIGZAG

from
MOONFLEET
by
J. MEADE FALKNER

John Meade Falkner was a remarkable man. All his working life he was an important industrialist: but he was also a busy scholar – an archeologist, a folklorist, a medieval historian, with a deep knowledge of architecture and church music. And on top of all that, he wrote one of the best adventure stories ever written, Moonfleet. *It begins, in fact, as one of the best of all stories about smuggling, and then turns into an account of a quest for a great lost diamond, and of the excitements and tragedies that arise out of its discovery.*

John Trenchard, driven from home by his prim aunt, has gone to live with Elzevir Block, who is landlord of the "Why Not? Inn" and a smuggler. Elzevir's son has been killed during a battle between smugglers and excisemen by the cruel-minded magistrate, Maskew. While they are landing an assignment of contraband on a lonely beach, Elzevir's men discover Maskew hiding in some bushes: Elzevir stays behind, meaning to kill Maskew, but at that moment, soldiers appear on the cliff, John spoils Elzevir's aim, and Maskew drops dead – killed by a stray bullet from above.

Falkner, who lived from 1858 to 1932, also wrote a quite terrifying ghost story called The Lost Stradivarius.

T he white chalk was a bulwark between us and the foe; and though one or two of them loosed off their matchlocks, trying to get at us sideways, they could not even see their quarry, and 'twas only shooting at a venture. We were safe. But for how short a time! Safe for just so long as it should please the soldiers not to come down and take us, safe with a discharged pistol in our grasp, and a shot man lying at our feet.

Elzevir was the first to speak: "Can you stand, John? Is the bone broken?"

"I cannot stand," I said; "there is something gone in my leg, and I feel blood running down into my boot."

He knelt and rolled down the leg of my stocking; but though he only moved my foot ever so little, it caused me sharp pain, for feeling was coming back after the first numbness of the shot.

"They have broke the leg, though it bleeds little," Elzevir said. "We have no time to splice it here, but I will put a kerchief round, and while I wrap it, listen to how we lie, and then choose what we shall do."

I nodded, biting my lips hard to conceal the pain he gave me, and he went on: "We have a quarter of an hour before the Posse can get down to us. But come they will, and thou canst judge what chances we have to save liberty or life with that carrion lying by us" – and he jerked his thumb at Maskew – "though I am glad 'twas not my hand that sent him to his reckoning, and therefore do not blame thee if thou didst make me waste a charge in air. So one thing we can do is to wait here until they come, and I can account for a few of them before they shoot me down; but thou canst not fight with a broken leg, and they will take thee alive, and then there is a dance on air at Dorchester Jail."

I felt sick with pain and bitterly cast down to think that I was like to come so soon to such a vile end; so only gave a sigh, wishing heartily that Maskew were not dead, and that my leg were not broke, but that I was back at the *Why Not?*, or even hearing one of Dr. Sherlock's sermons in my aunt's parlor.

Elzevir looked down at me when I sighed, and seeing, I suppose, that I was sorrowful, tried to put a better face on a bad business. "Forgive me, lad," he said, "if I have spoke too roughly. There is yet another way that we may try; and if thou hadst but two whole legs, I would have tried it, but now 'tis little short of madness. And yet, if thou fear'st not, I will still try it. Just at the end of this flat ledge, farthest from where the bridle-path leads down, but not a hundred yards from where we stand, there is a sheep-track leading up the cliffs. It starts where the under-cliff dies back again into the chalk face, and climbs by slants and elbow-turns up to the top. The shepherds call it the Zigzag, and even sheep lose their footing on it; and of men I never heard but one had climbed it, and that was lander Jordan, when the Excise was on his heels, half a century back. But he that tries it stakes all on head and foot, and a wounded bird like thee may not dare that flight. Yet, if thou art content to hang thy life upon a hair, I will carry thee some way; and where there is no room to carry, thou must down on hands and knees and trail thy foot."

It was a desperate chance enough, but came as welcome as a patch of blue through lowering skies. "Yes," I said, "dear Master Elzevir, let us get to it quickly; and if we fall, 'tis far better to die upon the rocks below than to wait here for them to hale us off to jail." And with that I tried to stand, thinking I might go dot-and-carry, even with a broken leg. But 'twas no use, and down I sank with a groan. Then Elzevir caught me up, holding me in his arms, with my head looking over his back, and made off for the Zigzag. And as we slunk along, close to the cliff-side, I saw, between the brambles, Maskew lying with his face turned up to the morning sky. And there was the little red hole in the middle of his forehead, and a thread of blood that welled up from it and trickled off onto the sward.

It was a sight to stagger any man, and would have made me swoon perhaps, but that there was no time, for we were at the end of the under-cliff, and Elzevir set me down for a minute, before he buckled to his task. And 'twas a task that might cow the bravest, and when I looked upon the Zigzag, it seemed better to stay where we were and fall into the hands of the Posse than set foot on that awful way and fall upon the rocks below. For the Zigzag started off as a fair enough chalk path, but in a few paces narrowed down till it was but a whiter thread against the gray-white cliff-face, and afterwards turned sharply back, crossing a hundred feet direct above our heads. And then I smelt an evil stench, and looking about, saw the blown-out carcass of a rotting sheep lie close at hand.

"Faugh," said Elzevir, "tis a poor beast has lost his foot hold."

It was an ill omen enough, and I said as much, beseeching him to make his own way up the Zigzag and leave me where I was, for that they might have mercy on a boy.

"Tush!" he cried; "it is thy heart that fails thee, and 'tis too late now to change counsel. We have fifteen minutes yet to win or lose with, and if we gain the cliff-top in that time we shall have an hour's start, or more, for they will take all that to search the under-cliff. And Maskew, too, will keep them in check a little, while they try to bring the life back to so good a man. But if we fall, why, we shall fall together, and outwit their cunning. So shut thy eyes, and keep them tight until I bid thee open them." With that, he caught me up again, and I shut my eyes firm, rebuking myself for my faint-heartedness, and not telling him how much my foot hurt me.

In a minute, I knew from Elzevir's steps that he had left the turf and was upon the chalk. Now I do not believe that there were half a dozen men beside in England who would have ventured up that path, even free and untrammeled, and not a man in all the world to do it with a full-grown lad in his arms. Yet Elzevir made no bones of it, nor spoke a single word; only he went very slow, and I felt him scuffle with his foot as he set it forward, to make sure he was putting it down firm.

I said nothing, not wishing to distract him from his terrible task, and held my breath when I could, so that I might lie quieter in his arms. Thus he went on for a time that seemed without end, and yet was really but a minute or two; and by degrees I felt the wind, that we could scarce perceive at all on the under-cliff, blow fresher and cold on the cliffside. And then the path grew steeper and steeper, and Elzevir went slower and slower, till at last he spoke:

"John, I am going to stop; but open not thy eyes till I have set thee down and bid thee."

I did as bidden, and he lowered me gently, setting me on all-fours upon the path; and speaking again:

"The path is too narrow here for me to carry thee, and thou must creep around this corner on thy hands and knees. But have a care to keep thy outer hand near to the inner, and the balance of thy body to the cliff, for there is no room to dance hornpipes here. And hold thy eyes fixed on the chalk-wall, looking neither down nor seaward."

'Twas well he told me what to do, and well I did it; for when I opened my eyes, even without moving them from the cliffside, I saw that the ledge was little more than a foot wide, and that ever so little a lean of the body would dash me on the rocks below. So I crept on, but spent much time that was so precious in traveling those ten yards to take me around the first elbow of the path; for my foot was heavy and gave me fierce pain to drag, though I tried to mask it from Elzevir. And he, forgetting what I suffered, cried out, "Quicken thy pace, lad, if thou canst, the time is short." Now so frail is man's temper, that though he was doing more than any ever did to save another's life, and was all I had to trust to in the world; yet because he forgot my pain and bade me quicken, my choler rose, and I nearly gave him back an angry word, but thought better of it and kept it in.

Then he told me to stop, for that the way grew wider and he would pick me up again. But here was another difficulty, for the path was still so narrow and the cliff-wall so close that he could not take me up in his arms. So I lay flat on my face, and he stepped over me, setting his foot between my shoulders to do it; and then, while he knelt down upon the path, I climbed up from behind upon him, putting my arms around his neck; and so he bore me piggyback. I shut my eyes firm again, and thus we moved along another spell, mounting still and feeling the wind still freshening.

At length, he said that we were come to the last turn of the path, and he must set me down once more. So down upon his knees and hands he went, and I slid off behind, onto the ledge. Both were on all fours now: Elzevir first and I following. But as I crept along, I relaxed care for a moment, and my eyes wandered from the cliffside and looked down. And far below, I saw the blue sea twinkling like a dazzling mirror, and the gulls wheeling about the sheer chalk wall, and then I thought of that bloated carcass of a sheep that had fallen from this very spot perhaps, and in an instant felt a sickening qualm and swimming of the brain, and knew that I was giddy and must fall.

Then I called out to Elzevir, and he, guessing what had

come over me, cries to turn upon my side and press my belly to the cliff. And how he did it in such a narrow strait I know not; but he turned around, and lying down himself thrust his hand firmly in my back, pressing me closer to the cliff. Yet it was none too soon, for if he had not held me tight, I should have flung myself down in sheer despair to get quit of that dreadful sickness.

"Keep thine eyes shut, John," he said, "and count up numbers loud to me, that I may know thou art not turning faint." So I gave out, "One, two, three," and while I went on counting, heard him repeating to himself, though his words seemed thin and far off: "We must have taken ten minutes to get here, and in five more they will be on the under-cliff; and if we ever reach the top, who knows but they have left a guard! No, no, they will not leave a guard, for not a man knows of the Zigzag; and, if they knew, they would not guess that we should try it. We have but fifty yards to go to win, and now this cursed giddy fit has come upon the child, and he will fall and drag me with him; or they will see us from below, and pick us off like sitting guillemots against the cliff-face."

So he talked to himself, and all the while I would have given a world to pluck up heart and creep on farther; yet could not, for the deadly sweating fear that had hold of me. Thus I lay with my face to the cliff, and Elzevir pushing firmly in my back; and the thing that frightened me most was that there was nothing at all for the hand to take hold of, for had there been a piece of string, or even a thread of cotton, stretched along to give me a semblance of support, I think I could have done it; but there was only the cliff wall, sheer and white, against that narrowest way, with never cranny to put a finger into. The wind was blowing in fresh puffs, and though I did not open my eyes, I knew that it was moving the little tufts of bent grass, and the chiding cries of the gulls seemed to invite me to be done with fear and pain and broken leg, and fling myself off on to the rocks below.

Then Elzevir spoke. "John," he said, "there is no time to play the woman; another minute of this and we are lost. Pluck up thy courage, keep thy eyes to the cliff, and forward."

Yet I could not, but answered: "I cannot, I cannot; if I open my eyes, or move hand or foot, I shall fall on the rocks below."

He waited a second, and then said: "Nay, move thou must, and 'tis better to risk falling now, than fall for certain with another bullet in thee later on." And with that he shifted his hand from my back and fixed it in my coat-collar, moving backwards himself, and setting to drag me after him.

Now, I was so besotted with fright that I would not budge an inch, fearing to fall over if I opened my eyes. And Elzevir, for all he was so strong, could not pull a helpless lump backwards up that path. So he gave it up, leaving go hold on me with a groan; and at that moment there rose from the under-cliff below a sound of voices and shouting.

"By God, they are down already!" cried Elzevir, "and have found Maskew's body; it is all up; another minute and they will see us."

But so strange is the force of mind on body, and the power of a greater to master a lesser fear, that when I heard those voices from below, all fright of falling left me in a moment, and I could open my eyes without a trace of giddiness. So I began to move forward again on hands and knees. And Elzevir, seeing me, thought for a moment I had gone mad, and was dragging myself over the cliff, but then he saw how it was, and moved backwards himself before me, saying in a low voice, "Brave lad! Once creep around this turn, and I will pick thee up again. There is but fifty yards to go, and we shall foil these devils yet!"

Then we heard the voices again, but farther off, and not so loud; and knew that our pursuers had left the under-cliff and turned down onto the beach, thinking that we were hiding by the sea.

Five minutes later, Elzevir stepped on to the cliff top, with me upon his back.

"We have made something of this throw," he said, "and are safe for another hour, though I thought thy giddy head had ruined us."

Then he put me gently upon the springy turf and lay down himself upon his back, stretching his arms out straight on either side and breathing hard to recover from the task he had performed.

ARRIETTY IS SEEN

from
THE BORROWERS
by
MARY NORTON

They live under the floorboards, and the furnishings of their lives, and their food, are "borrowed" from the "human beans" who live above in the big house. The chest-of-drawers is made of matchboxes: the round table has been fashioned out of a pillbox: and on the fire, lit in an old cog wheel, soup is cooked in a silver thimble. This little family of borrowers consists of Pod and his wife Homily and their daughter Arrietty: they are the Clocks, for their home is under the grandfather clock. Their great fear is of being seen: and, in the passage below, Arrietty, venturing for the first time into the backyard, has indeed been seen. (You'll want to know that Eggletina was a borrower who appeared to have been eaten by a cat.)

Mary Norton (born in England in 1903) was near-sighted as a child, and her invention of the borrowers sprang out of her memory of that time, when she had to peer closely at things and imagined a race of tiny human beings living among the plants in the flowerbeds.

I t was an eye. Or it looked like an eye. Clear and bright like the color of the sky. An eye like her own, but enormous. A glaring eye. Breathless with fear, she sat up. And the eye blinked. A great fringe of lashes came curving down and flew up again out of sight. Cautiously, Arrietty moved her legs: she would slide noiselessly in among the grass stems and slither away down the bank.

"Don't move!" said a voice, and the voice, like the eye, was enormous, but, somehow, hushed – and hoarse like a surge of wind through the grating on a stormy night in March.

Arrietty froze. "So this is it," she thought, "the worst and most terrible thing of all: I have been 'seen'! Whatever happened to Eggletina will now, almost certainly, happen to me!"

There was a pause, and Arrietty, her heart pounding in her ears, heard the breath again drawn swiftly into the vast lungs. "Or," said the voice, whispering still, "I shall hit you with my ash stick."

Suddenly Arrietty became calm. "Why?" she asked. How strange her own voice sounded! Crystal thin and harebell clear, it tinkled on the air.

"In case," came the surprised whisper at last, "you ran toward me, quickly, through the grass... in case," it went on, trembling a little, "you scrabbled at me with your nasty little hands."

Arrietty stared at the eye; she held herself quite still. "Why?" she asked again, and again the word tinkled – icy cold it sounded this time, and needle sharp.

"Things do," said the voice. "I've seen them. In India."

Arrietty thought of her Gazetteer of the World. "You're not in India now," she pointed out.

"Did you come out of the house?"

"Yes," said Arrietty.

"From whereabouts in the house?"

Arrietty stared at the eye. "I'm not going to tell you," she said at last bravely.

"Then I'll hit you with my ash stick!"

"All right," said Arrietty, "hit me!"

"I'll pick you up and break you in half!"

Arrietty stood up. "All right," she said and took two paces forward.

There was a sharp gasp and an earthquake in the grass: he spun away from her and sat up. a great mountain in a green jersey. He had fair, straight hair and golden eyelashes. "Stay where you are!" he cried.

Arrietty stared up at him. So this was "the boy!" Breath less, she felt, and light with fear. "I guessed you were about nine," she gasped after a moment.

He flushed. "Well, you're wrong, I'm ten." He looked down at her, breathing deeply. "How old are you?"

"Fourteen," said Arrietty. "Next June," she added, watching him.

There was silence while Arrietty waited, trembling a little. "Can you read?" the boy said at last.

"Of course," said Arrietty. "Can't you?"

"No," he stammered. "I mean – yes. I mean I've just come from India."

"What's that got to do with it?" asked Arrietty.

"Well, if you're born in India, you're bilingual. And if you're bilingual, you can't read. Not so well."

Arrietty stared up at him: what a monster, she thought, dark against the sky.

"Do you grow out of it?" she asked.

He moved a little, and she felt the cold flick of his shadow.

"Oh, yes," he said, "it wears off. My sisters were bilingual; now they aren't a bit. They could read any of those books upstairs in the schoolroom."

"So could I," said Arrietty quickly, "if someone could hold them and turn the pages. I'm not a bit bilingual. I can read anything."

"Could you read out loud?"

"Of course," said Arrietty.

"Would you wait here while I run upstairs and get a book now?"

"Well," said Arrietty; she was longing to show off; then a startled look came into her eyes. "Oh –" she faltered.

"What's the matter?" The boy was standing up now. He towered above her.

"How many doors are there to this house?" She squinted up at him against the bright sunlight. He dropped on one knee.

"Doors?" he said. "Outside doors?"

"Yes."

"Well, there's the front door, the back door, the gun room door, the kitchen door, the scullery door... and the french windows in the drawing-room."

"Well, you see," said Arrietty, "my father's in the hall, by the front door, working. He... he wouldn't want to be disturbed."

"Working?" said the boy. "What at?"

"Getting material," said Arrietty, "for a scrubbing-brush."

"Then I'll go in the side door;" he began to move away, but turned suddenly and came back to her.

He stood a moment, as though embarrassed, and then he said: "Can you fly?"

"No," said Arrietty, surprised; "can you?"

His face became even redder. "Of course not," he said angrily; "I'm not a fairy!"

"Well, nor am I," said Arrietty, "nor is anybody. I don't believe in them."

He looked at her strangely. "You don't believe in them?"

"No," said Arrietty; "do you?"

"Of course not!"

Really, she thought, he is a very angry kind of boy. "My mother believes in them," she said, trying to appease him. "She thinks she saw one once. It was when she was a girl and lived with her parents behind the sandpile in the potting-shed."

He squatted down on his heels and she felt his breath on her face. "What was it like?" he asked.

"About the size of a glowworm with wings like a butterfly. And it had a tiny little face, she said, all alight and moving like sparks, and tiny moving hands. Its face was changing all the time, she said, smiling and sort of shimmering. It seemed to be talking, she said, very quickly – but you couldn't hear a word."

"Oh," said the boy, interested. After a moment he asked: "Where did it go?"

"It just went," said Arrietty. "When my mother saw it, it seemed to be caught in a cobweb. It was dark at the time. About five o'clock on a winter's evening. After tea."

"Oh," he said again and picked up two petals of cherry-blossom which he folded together like a sandwich and ate slowly. "Supposing," he said, staring past her at the wall of the house, "you saw a little man, about as tall as a pencil, with a blue patch in his trousers, halfway up a window curtain, carrying a doll's teacup – would you say it was a fairy?"

"No," said Arrietty, "I'd say it was my father."

"Oh," said the boy, thinking this out, "does your father have a blue patch on his trousers?"

"Not on his best trousers. He does on his borrowing ones."

"Oh," said the boy again. He seemed to find it a safe sound, as lawyers do. "Are there many people like you?"

"No," said Arrietty. "None. We're all different."

"I mean as small as you?"

Arrietty laughed. "Oh, don't be silly!" she said. "Surely

you don't think there are many people in the world your size?"

"There are more my size than yours," he retorted.

"Honestly –" began Arrietty helplessly and laughed again. "Do you really think – I mean, whatever sort of a world would it be? Those great chairs... fancy if you had to make chairs that size for everyone? And the stuff for their clothes... miles and miles of it... tents of it... and the sewing! And their great houses, reaching up so you can hardly see the ceilings... the *food* they eat... great, smoking mountains of it, huge bogs of stew and soup and stuff."

"Don't you eat soup?" asked the boy.

"Of course we do," laughed Arrietty. "My father had an uncle who had a little boat which he rowed around in the stockpot picking up flotsam and jetsam. Once he was nearly shipwrecked on a chunk of submerged shinbone. He lost his oars and the boat sprang a leak, but he flung a line over the pot handle and pulled himself alongside the rim. But all that stock – fathoms of it! And the size of the stockpot! I mean, there wouldn't be enough stuff in the world to go around after a bit! That's why my father says it's a good thing they're dying out... just a few, my father says, that's all we need – to keep us. Otherwise, he says, the whole thing gets" – Arrietty hesitated trying to remember the word – "exaggerated, he says –"

"What do you mean," asked the boy, "'to keep us?'"

So Arrietty told him about borrowing – how difficult it was and how dangerous.

ALONG THE
YELLOW BRICK
ROAD

from
THE WIZARD OF OZ
by
L. FRANK BAUM

A long and risky journey, with strange men and women (or just strange creatures) encountered on the way… That's the shape of the story in a great many children's classics, including a number of those that provide the passages in this book. The Wizard of Oz *is one of the best of them. It was published in 1899. Dorothy lives on a farm in Kansas until a tornado, known locally as a twister, blows her and her little dog Toto*

into an entirely new, and as it turns out magical, world. To get back to Kansas, she must travel to Oz and appeal to the great Wizard: and setting out along the yellow brick road, she's already met the Scarecrow, who decides to come with her because he hopes the Wizard might give him brains, which he's very aware of lacking. They spend the night in a cottage before continuing the journey.

Baum wrote fourteen Oz books altogether (he took the name Oz from the label on the drawer of his filing cabinet, O-Z). They're full of odd characters ("real Ozzy," one young reader called them), like Mr. H.M. Woggle-Bug (H.M. standing for Highly Magnified) and Tiktok the mechanical man, who has to be wound up regularly and whose mechanism is guaranteed to work perfectly for a thousand years.

W hen Dorothy awoke, the sun was shining through the trees, and Toto had long been out chasing birds around her. There was the Scarecrow, still standing patiently in his corner, waiting for her.

"We must go and search for water," she said to him.

"Why do you want water?" he asked.

"To wash my face clean after the dust of the road, and to drink, so the dry bread will not stick in my throat."

"It must be inconvenient to be made of flesh," said the Scarecrow, thoughtfully, "for you must sleep, and eat, and drink. However, you have brains, and it is worth a lot of bother to be able to think properly."

They left the cottage and walked through the trees until they found a little spring of clear water, where Dorothy drank and bathed and ate her breakfast. She saw there was not much bread left in the basket, and the girl was thankful the Scarecrow did not have to eat anything, for there was scarcely enough for herself and Toto for the day.

When she had finished her meal and was about to go back to the road of yellow brick, she was startled to hear a deep groan near by.

"What was that?" she asked, timidly.

"I cannot imagine," replied the Scarecrow; "but we can go and see."

Just then, another groan reached their ears, and the sound seemed to come from behind them. They turned and walked through the forest a few steps, when Dorothy discovered something shining in a ray of sunshine that fell between the trees. She ran to the place and then stopped short, with a cry of surprise.

One of the big trees had been partly chopped through, and standing beside it, with an uplifted ax in his hands, was a man made entirely of tin. His head and arms and legs were jointed upon his body, but he stood perfectly motionless as if he could not stir at all.

Dorothy looked at him in amazement, and so did the Scarecrow, while Toto barked sharply and made a snap at the tin legs, which hurt his teeth.

"Did you groan?" asked Dorothy.

"Yes," answered the tin man, "I did. I've been groaning for more than a year, and no one has ever heard me before or come to help me."

"What can I do for you?" she inquired softly, for she was moved by the sad voice in which the man spoke.

"Get an oil-can and oil my joints," he answered. "They are rusted so badly that I cannot move them at all; if I am well oiled, I shall soon be all right again. You will find an oil-can on a shelf in my cottage."

Dorothy at once ran back to the cottage and found the oil-can, and then she returned and asked, anxiously, "Where are your joints?"

"Oil my neck, first," replied the Tin Woodman. So she oiled it, and as it was quite badly rusted, the Scarecrow took hold of the tin head and moved it gently from side to side until it worked freely, and then the man could turn it himself.

"Now oil the joints in my arms," he said. And Dorothy oiled them, and the Scarecrow bent them carefully until they were quite free from rust and as good as new.

The Tin Woodman gave a sigh of satisfaction and lowered his ax, which he leaned against the tree.

"This is a great comfort," he said. "I have been holding that ax in the air ever since I rusted, and I'm glad to be able to put it down at last. Now, if you will oil the joints of my legs, I shall be all right once more."

So they oiled his legs until he could move them freely; and he thanked them again and again for his release, for he seemed a very polite creature, and very grateful.

"I might have stood there always if you had not come along," he said; "so you have certainly saved my life. How did you happen to be here?"

"We are on our way to the Emerald City, to see the great Oz," she answered, "and we stopped at your cottage to pass the night."

"Why do you wish to see Oz?" he asked.

"I want him to send me back to Kansas; and the Scarecrow wants him to put a few brains into his head," she replied.

The Tin Woodman appeared to think deeply for a moment. Then he said:

"Do you suppose Oz could give me a heart?"

"Why, I guess so," Dorothy answered. "It would be as easy as to give the Scarecrow brains."

"True," the Tin Woodman returned. "So, if you will allow me to join your party, I will also go to the Emerald City and ask Oz to help me."

"Come along," said the Scarecrow heartily; and Dorothy added that she would be pleased to have his company. So the Tin Woodman shouldered his ax, and they all passed through the forest until they came to the road that was paved with yellow brick.

The Tin Woodman had asked Dorothy to put the oil-can in her basket. "For," he said, "if I should get caught in the rain, and rust again, I would need the oil-can badly."

It was a bit of good luck to have their new comrade join the party, for soon after they had begun their journey again, they came to a place where the trees and branches grew so thick over the road that the travelers could not pass. But the Tin Woodman set to work with his ax and chopped so well that soon he cleared a passage for the entire party.

Dorothy was thinking so earnestly as they walked along that she did not notice when the Scarecrow stumbled into a hole and rolled over to the side of the road. Indeed, he was obliged to call to her to help him up again.

"Why didn't you walk around the hole?" asked the Tin Woodman.

"I don't know enough," replied the Scarecrow cheerfully. "My head is stuffed with straw, you know, and that is why I am going to Oz to ask him for some brains."

"Oh, I see," said the Tin Woodman. "But, after all, brains are not the best things in the world."

"Have you any?" inquired the Scarecrow.

"No, my head is quite empty," answered the Woodman; "but once I had brains, and a heart also; so, having tried them both, I should much rather have a heart."

"And why is that?" asked the Scarecrow.

"I will tell you my story, and then you will know."

So, while they were walking through the forest, the Tin Woodman told the following story:

"I was born the son of a woodman who chopped down trees in the forest and sold the wood for a living. When I grew up, I too became a woodchopper; and after my father died, I took care of my old mother as long as she lived. Then I made up my mind that, instead of living alone, I would marry, so that I might not become lonely.

"There was one of the Munchkin girls who was so beautiful that I soon grew to love her with all my heart. She, on her part, promised to marry me as soon as I could earn enough money to build a better house for her; so I set to work harder than ever. But the girl lived with an old woman who did not want her to marry anyone, for she was so lazy she wished the girl to remain with her and do the cooking and the housework. So the old woman went to the Wicked Witch of the East and promised her two sheep and a cow if she would prevent the marriage. Thereupon the Wicked Witch enchanted my ax, and when I was chopping away at my best one day, for I was anxious to get the new house and my wife as soon as possible, the ax slipped all at once and cut off my left leg.

"This at first seemed a great misfortune, for I knew a one-legged man could not do very well as a woodchopper. So I went to a tinsmith and had him make me a new leg out of tin. The leg worked very well, once I was used to it; but my action angered the Wicked Witch of the East, for she had promised the old woman I should not marry the pretty Munchkin girl. When I began chopping again, my ax slipped and cut off my right leg. Again I went to the tinner, and again he made me a leg out of tin. After this, the enchanted ax cut off my arms, one after the other; but, nothing daunted, I had them replaced with tin ones. The Wicked Witch then made the ax slip and cut off my head, and at first I thought that was the end of me. But the tinsmith happened to come along, and he made me a new head out of tin.

"I thought I had beaten the Wicked Witch then, and I worked harder than ever; but I little knew how cruel my enemy could be. She thought of a new way to kill my love for the beautiful Munchkin maiden, and made my ax slip again, so that it cut right through my body, splitting me into two halves. Once more, the tinsmith came to my help and made me a body of tin, fastening my tin arms and legs and head to it, by means of joints, so that I could move around as well as ever. But, alas! I had now no heart, so that I lost all my love for the Munchkin girl and did not care whether I married her not. I suppose she is still living with the old woman, waiting for me to come after her.

"My body shone so brightly in the sun that I felt very proud of it, and it did not matter now if my ax slipped, for it could not cut me. There was only one danger – that my joints would rust; but I kept an oil-can in my cottage and took care to oil myself whenever I needed it. However, there came a day when I forgot to do this, and, being caught in a rainstorm, before I thought of the danger my joints had rusted, and I was left to stand in the woods until you came to help me. It was a terrible thing to undergo, but during the year I stood there, I had time to think that the greatest loss I had known was the loss of my heart. While I was in love, I was the happiest man on earth; but no one can love who has not a heart, and so I am resolved to ask Oz to give me one. If he does, I will go back to the Munchkin maiden and marry her."

Both Dorothy and the Scarecrow had been greatly interested in the story of the Tin Woodman, and now they knew why he was so anxious to get a new heart.

"All the same," said the Scarecrow, "I shall ask for brains instead of a heart; for a fool would not know what to do with a heart if he had one."

"I shall take the heart," returned the Tin Woodman, "for brains do not make one happy, and happiness is the best thing in the world."

Dorothy did not say anything, for she was puzzled to know which of her two friends was right, and she decided if she could only get back to Kansas and Aunt Em, it did not matter so much whether the Woodman had no brains and the Scarecrow had no heart, or each got what he wanted.

What worried her most was that the bread was nearly gone, and another meal for herself and Toto would empty the basket. To be sure, neither the Woodman nor the Scarecrow ever ate anything, but she was not made of tin nor straw, and could not live unless she was fed.

All this time, Dorothy and her companions had been walking through the thick woods. The road was still paved with yellow bricks, but these were much covered by dried branches and dead leaves from the trees, and the walking was not at all good.

There were few birds in this part of the forest, for birds love the open country where there is plenty of sunshine; but now and then, there came a deep growl from some wild animal hidden among the trees. These sounds made the little girl's heart beat fast, for she did not know what made them; but Toto knew, and he walked close to Dorothy's side and did not even bark in return.

"How long will it be," the child asked of the Tin Woodman, "before we are out of the forest?"

"I cannot tell," was the answer, "for I have never been to the Emerald City. But my father went there once, when I was a boy, and he said it was a long journey through a dangerous country, although nearer to the city where Oz dwells, the country is beautiful. But I am not afraid so long as I have my oil-can, and nothing can hurt the Scarecrow, while you bear upon your forehead the mark of the good Witch's kiss, and that will protect you from harm."

"But Toto!" said the girl anxiously. "What will protect him?"

"We must protect him ourselves, if he is danger," replied the Tin Woodman.

Just as he spoke, there came from the forest a terrible roar, and the next moment a great Lion bounded into the road. With one blow of his paw, he sent the Scarecrow spinning over and over to the edge of the road, and then he struck the Tin Woodman with his sharp claws. But, to the Lion's surprise, he could make no impression on the tin, although the Woodman fell over in the road and lay still.

Little Toto, now that he had an enemy to face, ran barking toward the Lion, and the great beast had opened his mouth to bite the dog, when Dorothy, fearing Toto would be killed, and heedless of the danger, rushed forward and slapped the Lion upon his nose as hard as she could, while she cried out:

"Don't you dare to bite Toto! You ought to be ashamed of yourself, a big beast like you, to bite a poor little dog!"

"I didn't bite him," said the Lion, as he rubbed his nose with his paw where Dorothy had hit it.

"No, but you tried to," she retorted. "You are nothing but a big coward."

"I know it," said the Lion, hanging his head in shame. "I've always known it. But how can I help it?"

"I don't know, I'm sure. To think of your striking a stuffed man, like the poor Scarecrow!"

"Is he stuffed?" asked the Lion in surprise, as he watched her pick up the Scarecrow and set him upon his feet, while she patted him into shape again.

"Of course he's stuffed," replied Dorothy, who was still angry.

"That's why he went over so easily," remarked the Lion.

"It astonished me to see him whirl around so. Is the other one stuffed also?"

"No," said Dorothy, "he's made of tin." And she helped the Woodman up again.

"That's why he nearly blunted my claws," said the Lion. "When they scratched against the tin, it made a cold shiver run down my back. What is that little animal you are so tender of?"

"He is my dog, Toto," answered Dorothy.

"Is he made of tin, or stuffed?" asked the Lion.

"Neither. He's a – a – a meat dog," said the girl.

"Oh! He's a curious animal and seems remarkably small, now that I look at him. No one would think of biting such a little thing, except a coward like me," continued the Lion sadly.

"What makes you a coward?" asked Dorothy, looking at

the great beast in wonder, for he was as big as a small horse.

"It's a mystery," replied the Lion. "I suppose I was born that way. All the other animals in the forest naturally expect me to be brave, for the Lion is everywhere thought to be the King of Beasts. I learned that if I roared very loudly every living thing was frightened and got out of my way. Whenever I've met a man, I've been awfully scared; but I just roared at him, and he has always run away as fast as he could go. If the elephants and the tigers and the bears had ever tried to fight me, I should have run myself – I'm such a coward; but just as soon as they hear me roar, they all try to get away from me, and of course I let them go."

"But that isn't right. The King of Beasts shouldn't be a coward," said the Scarecrow.

"I know it," returned the Lion, wiping a tear from his eye with the tip of his tail. "It is my great sorrow and makes my life very unhappy. But whenever there is a danger, my heart begins to beat fast."

"Perhaps you have heart disease," said the Tin Woodman.

"It may be," said the Lion.

"If you have," continued the Tin Woodman, "you ought to be glad, for it proves you have a heart. For my part, I have no heart; so I cannot have heart disease."

"Perhaps," said the Lion thoughtfully, "if I had no heart, I should not be a coward."

"Have you brains?" asked the Scarecrow.

"I suppose so. I've never looked to see," replied the Lion.

"I am going to the great Oz to ask him to give me some,"

remarked the Scarecrow, "for my head is stuffed with straw."

"And I am going to ask him to give me a heart," said the Woodman.

"And I am going to ask him to send Toto and me back to Kansas," added Dorothy.

"Do you think Oz could give me courage?" asked the Cowardly Lion.

"Just as easily as he could give me brains," said the Scarecrow.

"Or give me a heart," said the Tin Woodman.

"Or send me back to Kansas," said Dorothy.

"Then, if you don't mind, I'll go with you," said the Lion, "for my life is simply unbearable without a bit of courage."

"You will be very welcome," answered Dorothy, "for you will help to keep away the other wild beasts. It seems to me they must be more cowardly than you are if they allow you to scare them so easily."

"They really are," said the Lion, "but that doesn't make me any braver; and as long as I know myself to be a coward, I shall be unhappy."

So once more, the little company set off upon the journey, the Lion walking with stately strides at Dorothy's side. Toto did not approve this new comrade at first, for he could not forget how nearly he had been crushed between the Lion's great jaws; but after a time, he became more at ease, and presently Toto and the Cowardly Lion had grown to be good friends.

During the rest of that day, there was no other adventure to mar the peace of their journey. Once, indeed, the Tin Woodman stepped upon a beetle that was crawling along the road, and killed the poor little thing. This made the Tin Woodman very unhappy, for he was always careful not to hurt any living creature; and as he walked along, he wept several tears of sorrow and regret. These tears ran slowly down his face and over the hinges of his jaw, and there they rusted. When Dorothy presently asked him a question, the Tin Woodman could not open his mouth, for his jaws were tightly rusted together. He became greatly frightened at this and made many motions to Dorothy to relieve him, but she could not understand. The Lion was also puzzled to know what was wrong. But the Scarecrow seized the oil-can from Dorothy's basket and oiled the Woodman's jaws, so that after a few moments, he could talk as well as before.

"This will serve me a lesson," said he, "to look where I step. For if I should kill another bug or beetle, I should surely cry again, and crying rusts my jaws so that I cannot speak."

Thereafter he walked very carefully, with his eyes on the road, and when he saw a tiny ant toiling by, he would step over it, so as not to harm it. The Tin Woodman knew very well he had no heart, and therefore he took great care never to be cruel or unkind to anything.

"You people with hearts," he said, "have something to guide you and need never do wrong; but I have no heart, and so I must be very careful. When Oz gives me a heart of course, I needn't mind so much."

THE ELEPHANT'S CHILD

from
JUST SO STORIES
by
RUDYARD KIPLING

Rudyard Kipling, who lived from 1865 to 1936, spoke the Just So Stories *before ever he wrote them down; the audience for the earliest of them being his small daughter, Josephine. Most (there are twelve) offer extravagant and comical explanations of the physical characteristics of animals. We learn how the Camel got his hump, how the Rhinoceros got his skin, and (in the story below, written in 1889 when the whole Kipling family was in Africa) how the Elephant got his trunk. These tall tales can be read silently; but they cry out to be spoken and offer the reader-aloud a field-day (or, of course, if it's bedtime, a field-night).*

I n the High and Far-Off Times, the Elephant, O Best Beloved, had no trunk. He had only a blackish, bulgy nose, as big as a boot, that he could wriggle about from side to side; but he couldn't pick up things with it. But there was one Elephant – a new Elephant – an Elephant's Child – who was full of 'satiable curtiosity, and that means he asked ever so many questions. *And* he lived in Africa, and he filled all Africa with his 'satiable curtiosities. He asked his tall aunt, the Ostrich, why her tail-feathers grew just so, and his tall aunt the Ostrich spanked him with her hard, hard claw. He asked his tall uncle, the Giraffe, what made his skin spotty, and his tall uncle, the Giraffe, spanked him with his hard, hard hoof. And still he was full of 'satiable curtiosity! He asked his broad aunt, the Hippopotamus, why her eyes were red, and his broad aunt, the Hippopotamus, spanked him with her broad, broad hoof; and he asked his hairy uncle, the Baboon, why melons tasted just so, and his hairy uncle, the Baboon, spanked him with his hairy, hairy paw. And *still* he was full of 'satiable curtiosity! He asked questions about everything that he saw, or heard, or felt, or smelt, or touched, and all his uncles and his aunts spanked him. And still he was full of 'satiable curtiosity!

One fine morning in the middle of the Precession of the Equinoxes, this 'satiable Elephant's Child asked a new fine question that he had never asked before. He asked, "What does the Crocodile have for dinner?" Then everybody said, "Hush!" in a loud and dretful tone, and they spanked him immediately and directly, without stopping, for a long time.

By and by, when that was finished, he came upon Kolokolo Bird sitting in the middle of a wait-a-bit thorn-bush, and he said, "My father has spanked me, and my mother has spanked me; all my aunts and uncles have spanked me for my 'satiable curtiosity; and *still* I want to know what the Crocodile has for dinner!"

Then Kolokolo Bird said, with a mournful cry, "Go to the banks of the great gray-green, greasy Limpopo River, all set about with fever-trees, and find out."

That very next morning, when there was nothing left of the Equinoxes, because the Precession had preceded according to precedent, this 'satiable Elephant's Child took a hundred pounds of bananas (the little short red kind), and seventeen melons (the greeny-crackly kind), and said to all his dear families, "Goodbye. I am going to the great gray-green, greasy Limpopo River, all set about with fever-trees, to find out what the Crocodile has for dinner." And they all spanked him once more for luck, though he asked them most politely to stop.

Then he went away, a little warm, but not at all aston-ished, eating melons, and throwing the rind about, because he could not pick it up.

He went from Graham's Town to Kimberley, and from Kimberley to Khama's Country, and from Khama's Country he went east by north, eating melons all the time, till at last he came to the banks of the great gray-green, greasy Limpopo River, all set about with fever-trees, precisely as

Kolokolo Bird had said.

Now you must know and understand, O Best Beloved, that till that very week, and day, and hour, and minute, this 'satiable Elephant's Child had never seen a Crocodile, and did not know what one was like. It was all his 'satiable curtiosity.

The first thing that he found was a Bi-Colored-Python-Rock-Snake curled around a rock.

"'Scuse me," said the Elephant's Child most politely, "but have you seen such a thing as a Crocodile in these promiscuous parts?"

"*Have* I seen a Crocodile?" said the Bi-Colored-Python-Rock-Snake, in a voice of dretful scorn. "What will you ask me next?"

"'Scuse me," said the Elephant's Child, "but could you kindly tell me what he has for dinner?"

Then the Bi-Colored-Python-Rock-Snake uncoiled himself very quickly from the rock and spanked the Elephant's Child with his scalesome, flailsome tail.

"That is odd," said the Elephant's Child, "because my father and my mother, and my uncle and my aunt, not to mention my other aunt, the Hippopotamus, and my other uncle, the Baboon, have all spanked me for my 'satiable curtiosity – and I suppose this is the same thing."

So he said good-bye very politely to the Bi-Colored-Python-Rock-Snake, and helped to coil him up on the rock again, and went on, a little warm, but not at all astonished, eating melons, and throwing the rind about, because he could not pick it up, till he trod on what he thought was a log of wood at the very edge of the great gray-green, greasy Limpopo River, all set about with fever-trees.

But it was really the Crocodile, O Best Beloved, and the Crocodile winked one eye – like this!

"'Scuse me," said the Elephant's Child most politely, "but do you happen to have seen a Crocodile in these promiscuous parts?"

Then the Crocodile winked the other eye and lifted half his tail out of the mud; and the Elephant's Child stepped back most politely, because he did not wish to be spanked again.

"Come hither, Little One," said the Crocodile. "Why do you ask such things?"

"'Scuse me," said the Elephant's Child most politely, "but my father has spanked me, my mother has spanked me, not to mention my tall aunt, the Ostrich, and my tall uncle, the Giraffe, who can kick ever so hard, as well as my broad aunt, the Hippopotamus, and my hairy uncle, the Baboon, *and* including the Bi-Colored-Python-Rock-Snake, with the scalesome, flailsome tail, just up the bank, who spanks harder than any of them; and *so*, if it's quite all the same to you, I don't want to be spanked any more."

"Come hither, Little One," said the Crocodile, "for I am the Crocodile," and he wept crocodile-tears to show it was quite true.

Then the Elephant's Child grew all breathless, and panted, and kneeled down on the bank and said, "You are the very person I have been looking for all these long days.

Will you please tell me what you have for dinner?"

"Come hither, Little One," said the Crocodile, "and I'll whisper."

Then the Elephant's Child put his head down close to the Crocodile's musky, tusky mouth, and the Crocodile caught him by his little nose, which up to that very week, day, hour, and minute, had been no bigger than a boot, though much more useful.

"I think," said the Crocodile – and he said it between his teeth, like this – "I think today I will begin with Elephant's Child!"

At this, O Best Beloved, the Elephant's Child was much annoyed, and he said, speaking through his nose, like this, "Led go! You are hurtig be!"

Then the Bi-Colored-Python-Rock-Snake scuffled down from the bank and said, "My young friend, if you do not now, immediately and instantly, pull as hard as ever you can, it is my opinion that your acquaintance in the large-pattern leather ulster" (and by this he meant the Crocodile) "will jerk you into yonder limpid stream before you can say Jack Robinson."

This is the way Bi-Colored-Python-Rock-Snakes always talk.

Then the Elephant's Child sat back on his little haunches, and pulled, and pulled, and pulled, and his nose began to stretch. And the Crocodile floundered into the water, making it all creamy with great sweeps of his tail, and *he* pulled, and pulled, and pulled.

And the Elephant's Child's nose kept on stretching; and the Elephant's Child spread all his little four legs and pulled, and pulled, and pulled, and his nose kept on stretching; and the Crocodile threshed his tail like an oar, and *he* pulled, and pulled, and pulled, and at each pull the Elephant's Child's nose grew longer and longer – and it hurt him hijjus.

Then the Elephant's Child felt his legs slipping, and he said through his nose, which was now nearly five feet long, "This is too butch for be!"

Then the Bi-Colored-Python-Rock-Snake came down from the bank and knotted himself in a double-clove-hitch around the Elephant's Child's hind legs and said, "Rash and inexperienced traveler, we will now seriously devote ourselves to a little high tension, because if we do not, it is my impression that yonder self-propelling man-of-war with the armor-plated upper deck" (and by this, O Best Beloved, he meant the Crocodile) "will permanently vitiate your future career."

That is the way all Bi-Colored-Python-Rock-Snakes always talk.

So he pulled, and the Elephant's Child pulled, and the Crocodile pulled; but the Elephant's Child and the Bi-Colored-Python-Rock-Snake pulled hardest; and at last, the Crocodile let go of the Elephant's Child's nose with a plop that you could hear all up and down the Limpopo.

Then the Elephant's Child sat down most hard and sudden; but first he was careful to say "Thank you" to the Bi-Colored-Python-Rock-Snake; and next he was kind to his poor pulled nose, and wrapped it all up in cool banana leaves and hung it in the great gray-green, greasy Limpopo to cool.

"What are you doing that for?" said the Bi-Colored-Python-Rock-Snake.

"'Scuse me," said the Elephant's Child, "but my nose is badly out of shape, and I am waiting for it to shrink."

"Then you will have to wait a long time," said the Bi-Colored-Python-Rock-Snake. "Some people do not know what is good for them."

The Elephant's Child sat there for three days waiting for his nose to shrink. But it never grew any shorter, and, besides, it made him squint. For, O Best Beloved, you will see and understand that the Crocodile had pulled it out into a really truly trunk, same as all Elephants have today.

At the end of the third day, a fly came and stung him on the shoulder, and before he knew what he was doing, he lifted up his trunk and hit that fly dead with the end of it.

"'Vantage number one!" said the Bi-Colored-Python-Rock-Snake. "You couldn't have done that with a mere-smear nose. Try and eat a little now."

Before he thought what he was doing, the Elephant's Child put out his trunk and plucked a large bundle of grass, dusted it clean against his forelegs, and stuffed it into his own mouth.

"'Vantage number two!" said the Bi-Colored-Python-Rock-Snake. "You couldn't have done that with a mere-smear nose. Don't you think the sun is very hot here?"

"It is," said the Elephant's Child, and before he thought what he was doing, he schlooped up a schloop of mud from the banks of the great gray-green, greasy Limpopo, and slapped it on his head, where it made a cool schloopy-sloshy mud cap all trickly behind his ears.

"'Vantage number three!" said the Bi-Colored-Python-Rock-Snake. "You couldn't have done that with a mere-smear nose. Now, how do you feel about being spanked again?"

"'Scuse me, said the Elephant's Child, "but I should not like it at all."

"How would you like to spank somebody?" said the Bi-Colored-Python-Rock-Snake.

"I should like it very much indeed," said the Elephant's Child.

"Well," said the Bi-Colored-Python-Rock-Snake, "you will find that new nose of yours very useful to spank people with."

"Thank you," said the Elephant's Child, "I'll remember that; and now I think I'll go home to all my dear families and try."

So the Elephant's Child went home across Africa frisking and whisking his trunk. When he wanted fruit to eat, he pulled fruit down from a tree, instead of waiting for it to fall as he used to do. When he wanted grass, he plucked grass up from the ground, instead of going on his knees as he used to do. When the flies bit him, he broke off the branch of a tree and used it as a fly-whisk; and he made himself a new, cool, slushy-squshy mud cap whenever the sun was hot. When he felt lonely walking through Africa, he sang to himself down his trunk, and the noise was louder than several brass bands. He went especially out of his way to find a broad Hippopotamus (she was no relation of his), and he spanked her very hard, to make sure that the Bi-Colored-Python-Rock-Snake had spoken the truth about his new trunk. The rest of the time, he picked up the melon rinds that he had dropped on his way to the Limpopo – for he was a Tidy Pachyderm.

One dark evening, he came back to all his dear families, and he coiled up his trunk and said, "How do you do?" They were very glad to see him and immediately said, "Come here and be spanked for your 'satiable curtiosity."

"Pooh," said the Elephant's Child. "I don't think you peoples know anything about spanking; but *I* do, and I'll show you."

Then he uncurled his trunk and knocked two of his dear brothers head over heels.

"O Bananas!" said they, "where did you learn that trick, and what have you done to your nose?"

"I got a new one from the Crocodile on the banks of the great gray-green, greasy Limpopo River," said the Elephant's Child. "I asked him what he had for dinner, and he gave me this to keep."

"It looks very ugly," said his hairy uncle, the Baboon.

"It does," said the Elephant's Child. "But it's very useful," and he picked up his hairy uncle, the Baboon, by one hairy leg and hove him into a hornet's nest.

Then that bad Elephant's Child spanked all his dear families for a long time, till they were very warm and greatly astonished. He pulled out his tall Ostrich aunt's tail feathers; and he caught his tall uncle, the Giraffe, by the hind leg and dragged him through a thorn bush; and he shouted at his broad aunt, the Hippopotamus, and blew bubbles into her ear when she was sleeping in the water after meals; but he never let anyone touch Kolokolo Bird.

At last, things grew so exciting that his dear families went off one by one in a hurry to the banks of the great gray-green, greasy Limpopo River, all set about with fever-trees, to borrow new noses from the Crocodile. When they came back, nobody spanked anybody any more; and ever since that day, O Best Beloved, all the Elephants you will ever see, besides all those that you won't, have trunks precisely like the trunk of the 'satiable Elephant's Child.

THE RANSOM
OF RED CHIEF

by
O. HENRY

O. Henry's real name was William Sidney Porter. He was born in North Carolina in 1862; worked in a drugstore, on a ranch, and in a bank; and died in 1910. The most important fact about him is that he wrote some six hundred short stories. At their best, they have an unmistakeable quality – they are witty and warm-hearted, and their endings come as a short surprise. Indeed, he was a master of what is called the "trick ending": and sometimes this totally unexpected twist in the tail of a story, this artfully concealed shock, is simply very entertaining, as it is in The Ransom of Red Chief. *But sometimes, as you will find if you dip into the fat book that contains all his stories, it is rather more than just entertaining.*

I t looked like a good thing: but wait till I tell you. We were down South, in Alabama – Bill Driscoll and myself – when this kidnapping idea struck us. It was, as Bill afterward expressed it, "during a moment of temporary mental apparition"; but we didn't find that out till later.

There was a town down there, as flat as a flannel-cake, and called Summit, of course. It contained inhabitants of as harmless and self-satisfied a class of peasantry as ever clustered around a maypole.

Bill and me had a joint capital of about six hundred dollars, and we needed just two thousand dollars more to pull off a fraudulent real estate deal in western Illinois with. We talked it over on the front steps of the hotel. Family ties are strong in semirural communities, says we; therefore, and for other reasons, a kidnapping project ought to do better there than in the radius of newspapers that send reporters out in plain clothes to stir up talk about such things. We knew that Summit couldn't get after us with anything stronger than constables and, maybe, some lackadaisical bloodhounds and a diatribe or two in the local paper. So, it looked good.

We selected for our victim the only child of a prominent citizen named Ebenezer Dorset. The father was respectable and tight, and a stern, upright collection-plate passer and forecloser. The kid was a freckle-faced boy of nine, with hair the color of the magazine you buy at the newstand. Bill and me figured that Ebenezer would melt down a ransom of two thousand dollars in a flash. But wait till I tell you.

About two miles from Summit was a little mountain, covered with a dense cedar brake. On the rear elevation of this mountain was a cave. There we stored provisions.

One evening after sundown, we drove in a buggy past old Dorset's house. The kid was in the street, throwing rocks at a kitten on the opposite fence.

"Hey, little boy!" says Bill, "would you like to have a bag of candy and a nice ride?"

The boy catches Bill neatly in the eye with a piece of brick.

"That will cost the old man an extra five hundred dollars," says Bill, climbing over the wheel.

That boy put up a fight like a welterweight cinnamon bear; but, at last, we got him down in the bottom of the buggy and drove away. We took him up to the cave, and I hitched the horse in the cedar brake. After dark, I drove the buggy to the little village, three miles away, where we had rented it, and walked back to the mountain.

Bill was pasting court-plaster over the scratches and bruises on his features. There was a fire burning behind the big rock at the entrance of the cave, and the boy was watching a pot of boiling coffee, with two buzzard tail feathers stuck in his red hair. He points a stick at me when I come up, and says, "Ha! Cursed paleface, do you dare to enter the camp of Red Chief, the terror of the plains?"

"He's all right," says Bill, rolling up his pants and examining some bruises on his shins. "We're playing Indian. I'm Old Hank the Trapper, Red Chief's captive, and I'm to be scalped at daybreak. By Geronimo! that kid can kick hard."

Yes, sir, that boy seemed to be having the time of his life. The fun of camping out in a cave had made him forget that he was a captive himself. He immediately christened me Snake-eye, the Spy, and announced that, when his braves returned from the warpath, I was to be broiled at the stake at the rising of the sun.

Then we had supper; and he filled his mouth full of bacon and bread and gravy, and began to talk. He made a during-dinner speech something like this:

"I like this fine. I never camped out before; but I had a pet 'possum once, and I was nine last birthday. I hate to go to school. Rats ate up sixteen of Jimmy Talbot's aunt's speckled hen's eggs. Are there any real Indians in these woods? I want some more gravy. Does the trees moving make the wind blow? We had five puppies. What makes your nose so red, Hank? My father has lots of money. Are the stars hot? I whipped Ed Walker twice, Saturday. I don't like girls. You dassent catch toads unless with a string. Do oxen make any noise? Why are oranges round? Have you got beds to sleep on in this cave? Amos Murray has got six toes. A parrot can talk, but a monkey or fish can't. How many does it take to make twelve?"

Every few minutes he would remember that he was a pesky redskin, and pick up his stick rifle and tiptoe to the mouth of the cave to watch for the scouts of the hated paleface. Now and then, he would let out a war-whoop that made Old Hank the Trapper shiver. That boy had Bill terrorized from the start.

"Red Chief," says I to the kid, "would you like to go home?"

"Aw, what for?" says he. "I don't have any fun at home. I hate to go to school. I like to camp out. You won't take me back home again, Snake-eye, will you?"

"Not right away," says I. "We'll stay here in the cave awhile."

"All right!" says he. "That'll be fine. I never had such fun in all my life."

We went to bed about eleven o'clock. We spread down some wide blankets and quilts and put Red Chief between us. We weren't afraid he'd run away. He kept us awake for three hours, jumping up and reaching for his rifle and screeching, "Hist! Pard," in mine and Bill's ears, as the fancied crackle of a twig or the rustle of a leaf revealed to his young imagination the stealthy approach of the outlaw band. At last, I fell into a troubled sleep and dreamed that I had been kidnapped and chained to a tree by a ferocious pirate with red hair.

Just at daybreak, I was awakened by a series of awful screams from Bill. They weren't yells, or howls, or shouts, or whoops, or yawps, such as you'd expect from a manly set of vocal organs – they were simply indecent, terrifying, humiliating screams. It's an awful thing to hear a strong, desperate, fat man scream uncontrollably in a cave at daybreak.

I jumped up to see what the matter was. Red Chief was sitting on Bill's chest, with one hand twined in Bill's hair. In the other, he had a jackknife we used for slicing bacon; and he was industriously and realistically trying to take Bill's scalp, according to the sentence that had been pronounced upon him the evening before.

I got the knife away from the kid and made him lie down again. But, from that moment, Bill's spirit was broken. He laid down on his side of the bed, but he never closed an eye again in sleep as long as that boy was with us. I dozed off for a while, but along toward sun-up I remembered that Red Chief had said I was to be burned at the stake at the rising of the sun. I wasn't nervous or afraid; but I sat up and lit my pipe and leaned against a rock.

"What you getting up so soon for, Sam?" asked Bill.

"Me?" says I. "Oh, I got a kind of pain in my shoulder. I thought sitting up would rest it."

"You're a liar!" says Bill. "You're afraid. You was to be burned at sunrise, and you was afraid he'd do it. And he would, too, if he could find a match. Ain't it awful, Sam? Do you think anybody will pay our money to get a little imp like that back home?"

"Sure," said I. "A rowdy kid like that is just the kind that parents dote on. Now, you and the Chief get up and cook breakfast, while I go up on the top of this mountain and reconnoiter."

I went up on the peak of the little mountain and ran my eye over the vicinity. Over toward Summit, I expected to see the sturdy yeomanry of the village armed with scythes and pitch-forks beating the countryside for the dastardly kidnappers. But what I saw was a peaceful landscape dotted with one man plowing with a dun mule. Nobody was dragging the creek; no couriers dashed hither and yon, bringing tiding of no news to the distracted parents. "Perhaps," says I to myself, "it has not yet been discovered that the wolves have borne away the tender lambkin from the fold. Heaven help the wolves!" says I, and I went down the mountain to breakfast.

When I got to the cave, I found Bill backed up against the side of it, breathing hard, and the boy threatening to smash him with a rock half as big as a coconut.

"He put a red-hot boiled potato down my back," explained Bill, "and then mashed it with his foot; and I boxed his ears. Have you got a gun about you, Sam?"

I took the rock away from the boy and kind of patched up the argument. "I'll fix you," says the kid to Bill. "No man ever yet struck the Red Chief, but he got paid for it. You better beware!"

After breakfast, the kid takes a piece of leather with strings wrapped around it out of his pocket and goes outside the cave unwinding it.

"What's he up to now?" says Bill, anxiously. "You don't think he'll run away, do you, Sam?"

"No fear of it," says I. "He don't seem to be much of a homebody. But we've got to fix up some plan about the ransom. There don't seem to be much excitement around Summit on account of his disappearance; but maybe they haven't realized yet that he's gone. His folks may think he's spending the night with Aunt Jane or one of the neighbors.

Anyhow, he'll be missed today. Tonight we must get a message to his father demanding the two thousand dollars for his return."

Just then, we heard a kind of war-whoop, such as David might have emitted when he knocked out the champion Goliath. It was a sling that Red Chief had pulled out of his pocket, and he was whirling it around his head.

I dodged, and heard a heavy thud and a kind of a sigh from Bill, like a horse gives out when you take his saddle off. A rock the size of an egg had caught Bill just behind his left ear. He loosened himself all over and fell in the fire across the frying pan of hot water for washing the dishes. I dragged him out and poured cold water on his head for half an hour.

I went out and caught the boy and shook him until his freckles rattled.

"If you don't behave." says I, "I'll take you straight home. Now, are you going to be good, or not?"

"I was only funning," says he, sullenly. "I didn't mean to hurt Old Hank. But what did he hit me for? I'll behave, Snake-eye, if you won't send me home, and if you'll let me play the Black Scout today?"

"I don't know the game," says I. "That's for you and Mr. Bill to decide. He's your playmate for the day. I'm going away for a while, on business. Now, you come in and make friends with him and say you are sorry for hurting him, or home you go, at once."

I made him and Bill shake hands, and then I took Bill aside and told him I was going to Poplar Cove, a little village three miles from the cave, to find out what I could about how the kidnapping had been regarded in Summit. Also, I thought it best to send a peremptory letter to old man Dorset that day, demanding the ransom and dictating how it should be paid.

"You know, Sam," says Bill, "I've stood by you without batting an eye in earthquakes, fire, and flood – in poker games, dynamite outrages, police raids, train robberies, and cyclones. I never lost my nerve yet till we kidnapped that two-legged skyrocket of a kid. He's got me going. You won't leave me long with him, will you, Sam?"

"I'll be back some time this afternoon," says I. "You must keep the boy amused and quiet till I return. And now we'll write the letter to old Dorset."

Bill and I got paper and pencil and worked on the letter while the Red Chief, with a blanket wrapped around him, strutted up and down, guarding the mouth of the cave. Bill begged me tearfully to make the ransom fifteen hundred dollars instead of two thousand. "I ain't attempting," says he, "to decry the celebrated moral aspect of parental affection, but we're dealing with humans, and it ain't human for anybody to give up two thousand dollars for that forty-pound chunk of freckled wildcat. I'm willing to take a chance of fifteen hundred dollars. You can charge the difference up to me."

So, to relieve Bill, I acceded, and we collaborated a letter that ran this way:

We have your boy concealed in a place far from Summit. It is useless for you or the most skillful detectives to attempt to find him. Absolutely, the only terms on which you can have him restored to you are these: We demand fifteen hundred dollars in large bills for his return; the money to be left at midnight tonight at the same spot and in the same box as your reply – hereinafter described. If you agree to these terms, send your answer in writing by a solitary messenger tonight at half-past eight o'clock. After crossing Owl Creek on the road to Poplar Cove, there are three large trees about a hundred yards apart, close to the fence of the wheat field on the right-hand side. At the bottom of the fencepost, opposite the third tree, will be found a small pasteboard box.

The messenger will place the answer in this box and return immediately to Summit.

If you attempt any treachery or fail to comply with our demand as stated, you will never see your boy again.

If you pay the money demanded, he will be returned to you safe and well within three hours. These terms are final, and if you do not accede to them, no further communication will be attempted.

TWO DESPERATE MEN

I addressed this letter to Dorset and put it in my pocket. As I was about to start, the kid comes up to me and says:

"Aw, Snake-eye, you said I could play the Black Scout while you was gone."

"Play it, of course," says I. "Mr. Bill will play with you. What kind of game is it?"

"I'm the Black Scout," says Red Chief, "and I have to ride to the stockade to warn the settlers that the Indians are coming. I'm tired of playing Indian myself. I want to be the Black Scout."

"All right," says I. "It sounds like harmless enough to me. I guess Mr. Bill will help you foil the pesky savages."

"What am I to do?" asks Bill, suspiciously.

"You are the hoss," says Black Scout. "Get down on your hands and knees. How can I ride to the stockade without a hoss?"

"You'd better keep him interested," says I, "till we get the scheme going. Loosen up."

Bill gets down on his all fours, and a look comes in his eye, like a rabbit's when you catch it in a trap.

"How far is it to the stockade, kid?" he asks, in a husky manner of voice.

"Ninety miles," says the Black Scout. "And you have to hump yourself to get there on time. Whoa, now!"

The Black Scout jumps on Bill's back and digs his heels in his side.

"For heaven's sake," says Bill, "hurry back, Sam, as soon as you can. I wish we hadn't made the ransom note more than a thousand. Say, you quit kicking me, or I'll get up and warm you good."

I walked over to Poplar Cove and sat around the post office and store, talking with the chaw-bacons that came in to trade. One whiskerando says that he hears Summit is all upset on account of Elder Ebenezer Dorset's boy having been lost or stolen. That was all I wanted to know. I posted my letter surreptitiously and came away. The postmaster said the mail carrier would come by in an hour to take the mail to Summit.

When I got back to the cave, Bill and the boy were not to be found. I explored the vicinity of the cave and risked a yodel or two, but there was no response.

In about half an hour, I heard the bushes rustle, and Bill waddled out into the little glade in front of the cave. Behind him was the kid, stepping softly like a scout, with a broad grin on his face. Bill stopped, took off his hat, and wiped his face with a red handkerchief. The kid stopped about eight feet behind him.

"Sam," says Bill, "I suppose you'll think I'm a renegade, but I couldn't help it. I was rode the ninety miles to the stockade, not barring an inch. Then, when the settlers was rescued, I was given oats. Sand ain't a palatable substitute. And then, for an hour I had to try to explain to him why there was nothin' in holes, how a road can run both ways and what makes the grass green. I tell you, Sam, a human can only stand so much. I takes him by the neck of his clothes and drags him down the mountain. On the way he kicks my legs black-and-blue from the knees down; and I've got to have two or three bites on my thumb and hand cauterized."

"But he's gone" – continues Bill – "gone home. I showed him the road to Summit and kicked him about eight feet nearer there at one kick. I'm sorry we lose the ransom; but it was either that or Bill Driscoll to the madhouse."

Bill is puffing and blowing, but there is a look of indescribable peace and growing content on his rose-pink features.

"Bill," says I, "there isn't any heart disease in your family, is there?"

"No," says Bill, "nothing chronic except malaria and accidents. Why?"

"Then you might turn around," says I, "and have a look

behind you."

Bill turns and sees the boy, and loses his complexion and sits down plump on the ground and begins to pluck aimlessly at grass and little sticks. For an hour, I was afraid of his mind. And then I told him that my scheme was to put the whole job through immediately and that we would get the ransom and be off with it by midnight if old Dorset fell in with our position.

I had a scheme for collecting that ransom without danger of being caught by counterplots that ought to commend itself to professional kidnappers. The tree under which the answer was to be left – and the money later on – was close to the road fence with big, bare fields on all sides. If a gang of constables should be watching for anyone to come for the note, they could see him a long way off crossing the fields or in the road. But no, sirree! At half-past eight, I was up in that tree as well hidden as a tree toad, waiting for the messenger to arrive.

Exactly on time, a half-grown boy rides up the road on a bicycle, locates the pasteboard box at the foot of the fencepost, slips a folded piece of paper into it, and pedals away again back toward Summit.

I waited an hour and then concluded the thing was square. I slid down the tree, got the note, slipped along the fence till I struck the woods, and was back at the cave in another half an hour. I opened the note, got near the lantern, and read it to Bill. It was written with a pen in a crabbed hand, and the sum and substance of it was this:

TWO DESPERATE MEN:

Gentlemen: I received your letter today by post, in regard to the ransom you ask for the return of my son. I think you are a little high in your demands, and I hereby make you a counter-proposition, which I am inclined to believe you will accept. You bring Johnny home and pay me two hundred and fifty dollars in cash, and I agree to take him off your hands. You had better come at night, for the neighbors believe he is lost, and I couldn't be responsible for what they would do to anybody they saw bringing him back. Very respectfully,

EBENEZER DORSET

"Great Pirates of Penzance," says I, "of all the impudent –"

But I glanced at Bill, and hesitated. He had the most appealing look in his eyes I ever saw on the face of a dumb or a talking brute.

"Sam," says he, "what's two hundred and fifty dollars, after all? We've got the money. One more night of this kid will send me to a bed in Bedlam. Besides being a thorough gentleman, I think Mr. Dorset is a spendthrift for making us such a liberal offer. You ain't going to let the chance go, are you?"

"Tell you the truth, Bill," says I, "this little lamb has somewhat got on my nerves, too. We'll take him home, pay the ransom, and make our getaway."

We took him home that night. We got him to go by telling him that his father had bought a silver-mounted rifle and a pair of moccasins for him, and we were going to hunt bears the next day.

It was just twelve o'clock when we knocked at Ebenezer's front door. Just at the moment when I should have been abstracting the fifteen hundred dollars from the box under the tree, according to the original proposition, Bill was counting out two hundred and fifty dollars into Dorset's hand.

When the kid found out we were going to leave him at home, he started up a howl like a calliope and fastened himself as tight as a leech to Bill's leg. His father peeled him away gradually, like a mustard plaster.

"How long can you hold him?" asks Bill.

"I'm not as strong as I used to be, "says old Dorset, "but I think I can promise you ten minutes."

"Enough," says Bill. "In ten minutes, I shall cross the Central, Southern, and Middle Western states, and be legging it trippingly for the Canadian border."

And, as dark as it was, and as fat as Bill was, and as good a runner as I am, he was a good mile and a half out of Summit before I could catch up with him.

A NEW HOME

from
BLACK BEAUTY
by
ANNA SEWELL

Black Beauty: the autobiography of a horse *was published in 1877, and its author, Anna Sewell (an invalid who took seven years to write it, able to work only for a few sentences at a time), said what she hoped the book would do was "to induce kindness, sympathy, and an understanding treatment of horses." I had it read to me at school when I was very small, and have never forgotten how happy I felt when Black Beauty was in good hands, and how dismal when he passed to some cruel or careless owner. In the extract that follows, he's about to begin one of his more pleasant adventures, as a riding and carriage horse for Squire Gordon and his lady.*

Anna Sewell lived from 1820 to 1878. There was something wrong with her bones, and she could get about only in a pony cart. She died a few months after the book was published and never knew how enormously famous it became.

T he name of the coachman was John Manly; he had a wife and one little child, and they lived in the coachman's cottage, very near the stables.

The next morning, he took me into the yard and gave me a good grooming, and just as I was going into my box with my coat soft and bright, the Squire came in to look at me, and seemed pleased. "John," he said, "I meant to have tried the new horse this morning, but I have other business. You may as well take him a round after breakfast; go by the common and the Highwood, and back by the watermill and the river, that will show his paces."

"I will, sir," said John. After breakfast, he came and fitted me with a bridle. He was very particular in letting out and taking in the straps, to fit my head comfortably; then he brought the saddle, that was not broad enough for my back; he saw it in a minute and went for another, which fitted nicely. He rode me first slowly, then a trot, then a canter, and when we were on the common, he gave me a light touch with his whip, and we had a splendid gallop.

"Ho, ho! my boy," he said, as he pulled me up, "you would like to follow the hounds, I think."

As we came back through the Park, we met the Squire and Mrs. Gordon walking; they stopped, and John jumped off.

"Well, John, how does he go?"

"First-rate, sir," answered John, "he is as fleet as a deer and has a fine spirit, too: but the lightest touch of the rein will guide him. Down at the end of the common, we met one of those traveling carts hung all over with baskets, rugs, and such like; you know, sir, many horses will not pass those carts quietly; he just took a good look at it, and then went on as quiet and pleasant as could be. They were shooting rabbits near the Highwood, and a gun went off close by; he pulled up a little and looked, but did not stir a step to right or left. I just held the rein steady and did not hurry him, and it's my opinion he has not been frightened or ill-used while he was young."

"That's well," said the Squire, "I will try him myself tomorrow."

The next day, I was brought up for my master. I remembered my mother's counsel and my good old master's, and I tried to do exactly what he wanted me to do. I found he was a very good rider and thoughtful for his horse, too. When we came home, the lady was at the Hall door as he rode up.

"Well, my dear," she said, "how do you like him?"

"He is exactly what John said," he replied; "a pleasanter creature I never wished to mount. What shall we call him?"

"Would you like Ebony?" said she, "he is black as ebony."

"No, not Ebony."

"Will you call him Blackbird, like your uncle's old horse?"

"No, he is far handsomer than old Blackbird ever was."

"Yes," she said, "he is really quite a beauty, and he has such a sweet-tempered face and such a fine intelligent eye – what do you say to calling him Black Beauty?"

"Black Beauty – why, yes, I think that is a very good name. If you like, it shall be his name," and so it was.

John seemed very proud of me: he used to make my mane

and tail almost as smooth as a lady's hair, and he would talk to me a great deal; of course, I did not understand all he said, but I learned more and more to know what he *meant*, and what he wanted me to do. I grew very fond of him, he was so gentle and kind, he seemed to know just how a horse feels, and when he cleaned me, he knew the tender places, and the ticklish places; when he brushed my head, he went as carefully over my eyes as if they were his own, and never stirred up any ill-temper.

James Howard, the stable boy, was just as gentle and pleasant in his way, so I thought myself well off. There was another man who helped in the yard, but he had very little to do with Ginger and me.

A few days after this, I had to go out with Ginger in the carriage. I wondered how we should get on together; but except laying her ears back when I was led up to her, she behaved very well. She did her work honestly and did her full share, and I never wish to have a better partner in double harness. When we came to a hill, instead of slackening her pace, she would throw her weight right into the collar and pull away straight up. We had both the same sort of courage at our work, and John had oftener to hold us in than to urge us forward; he never had to use the whip with either of us; then our paces were much the same, and I found it very easy to keep step with her when trotting, which made it pleasant, and master always liked it when we kept step well, and so did John. After we had been out two or three times together, we grew quite friendly and sociable, which made me feel very much at home.

As for Merrylegs, he and I soon became great friends; he was such a cheerful, plucky, good-tempered little fellow that he was a favorite with everyone, and especially with Miss Jessie and Flora, who used to ride him about in the orchard, and have fine games with him and their little dog Frisky.

Our master had two horses that stood in another stable. One was Justice, a roan cob, used for riding, or for the luggage cart; the other was an old brown hunter, named Sir Oliver; he was past work now, but was a great favorite with the master, who gave him the run of the Park; he sometimes did a little light carting on the estate, or carried one of the young ladies when they rode out with their father; for he was very gentle and could be trusted with a child as well as Merrylegs. The cob was a strong, well-made, good-tempered horse, and we sometimes had a little chat in the paddock, but of course I could not be so intimate with him as with Ginger, who stood in the same stable.

I was quite happy in my new place, and if there was one thing that I missed, it must not be thought that I was discontented; all who had to do with me were good, and I had a light airy stable and the best of food. What more could I want? Why, liberty! For three years and a half of my life, I had had all the liberty I could wish for; but now, week after week, month after month, and no doubt year after year, I must stand up in a stable night and day except when I am wanted, and then I must be just as steady and quiet as any old horse who has worked twenty years. Straps here and straps there, a bit in my mouth, and blinkers over my eyes. Now, I am not complaining, for I know it must be so. I only mean to say that for a young horse full of strength and spirits who has been used to some large field or plain, where he can fling up his head, and toss up his tail and gallop away at full speed, then round and back again with a snort to his companions—I say it is hard never to have a bit more liberty to do as you like. Sometimes, when I have had less exercise than usual, I have felt so full of life and spring, that when John has taken me out to exercise, I really could not keep quiet; do what I would, it seemed as if I must jump, or dance, or prance, and many a good shake I know I must have given him, specially at the first; but he was always good and patient.

"Steady, steady, my boy," he would say; "wait a bit and we'll have a good swing, and soon get the tickle out of your feet." Then as soon as we were out of the village, he would give me a few miles at a spanking trot and then bring me back as fresh as before, only clear of the fidgets, as he called them. Spirited horses, when not enough exercised, are often called skittish, when it is only play; and some grooms will punish them, but our John did not, he knew it was only high spirits. Still, he had his own ways of making me understand by the tone of his voice or the touch of the rein. If he was very serious and quite determined, I always knew it by his voice, and that had more power with me than anything else, for I was very fond of him.

I ought to say that sometimes we had our liberty for a few hours; this used to be on fine Sundays in the summertime. The carriage never went out on Sundays, because the church was not far off.

It was a great treat to us to be turned out into the home paddock or the old orchard. The grass was so cool and soft to our feet; the air was so sweet, and the freedom to do as we liked was so pleasant; to gallop, to lie down, and roll over on our backs, or to nibble the sweet grass. Then it was a very good time for talking, as we stood together under the shade of the large chestnut tree.

One day, when Ginger and I were standing alone in the shade, we had a great deal of talk; she wanted to know all about my bringing up and breaking in, and I told her.

"Well," said she, "if I had had your bringing up, I might have been of as good a temper as you are, but now I don't believe I ever shall."

"Why not?" I said.

"Because it has been all so different with me," she replied; "I never had anyone, horse or man, that was kind to me, or that I cared to please; for in the first place, I was taken from my mother as soon as I was weaned and put with a lot of other young colts: none of them cared for me, and I cared for none of them. There was no kind master like yours to look after me, and talk to me, and bring me nice things to eat. The man that had the care of us never gave me a kind word in my life. I do not mean that he ill-used me, but that he did not care for us one bit further than to see that we had plenty to eat and shelter in the winter.

"A footpath ran through our field and very often the great boys passing through would fling stones to make us gallop. I was never hit, but one fine young colt was badly cut in the face, and I should think it would be a scar for life. We did not care for them, but of course it made us more wild, and we settled it in our minds that boys were our enemies.

"We had very good fun in the free meadows, galloping up and down and chasing each other round and round the field; then standing still under the shade of the trees. But when it came to breaking in, that was a bad time for me; several men came to catch me, and when at last they closed me in at one corner of the field, one caught me by the forelock, another caught me by the nose and held it so tight I could hardly draw my breath; then another took my underjaw in his hard hand and wrenched my mouth open, and so by force they got on the halter and the bar into my mouth; then one dragged me along by the halter, another flogging behind, and this was the first experience I had of men's kindness, it was all force; they did not give me a chance to know what they wanted. I was high bred and had a great deal of spirit, and was very wild, no doubt, and gave them I dare say plenty of trouble, but then it was dreadful to be shut up in a stall day after day instead of having my liberty, and I fretted and pined and wanted to get loose. You know yourself, it's bad enough when you have a kind master and plenty of coaxing, but there was nothing of that sort for me.

"There was one – the old master, Mr. Ryder, who I think could soon have brought me around and could have done anything with me, but he had given up all the hard part of the trade to his son and to another experienced man, and he only came at times to oversee. His son was a strong, tall, bold man; they called him Samson, and he used to boast that he had never found a horse that could throw him. There was no gentleness in him as there was in his father, but only hardness, a hard voice, a hard eye, a hard hand, and I felt from the first that what he wanted was to wear all the spirit out of me and just make me into a quiet, humble, obedient piece of horseflesh. 'Horseflesh!' Yes, that is all that he thought about," and Ginger stamped her foot as if the very thought of him made her angry.

She went on: "If I did not do exactly what he wanted, he would get put out and make me run around with that long rein in the training field till he had tired me out. I think he drank a good deal, and I am quite sure that the oftener he drank, the worse it was for me. One day, he had worked me hard in every way he could, and when I laid down, I was tired and miserable and angry; it all seemed so hard. The next morning, he came for me early and ran me around again for a long time. I had scarcely had an hour's rest, when he came again for me with a saddle and bridle and a new kind of bit. I could never quite tell how it came about; he had only just mounted me on the training ground, when something I did put him out of temper, and he chucked me hard with the rein. The new bit was very painful, and I reared up suddenly, which angered him still more, and he began to flog me. I felt my whole spirit set against him, and I began to kick and plunge, and rear as I had never done before, and we had a regular fight: for a long time, he stuck to the saddle and punished me cruelly with his whip and spurs, but my blood was thoroughly up, and I cared for nothing he could do if only I could get him off. At last, after a terrible struggle, I threw him off backwards. I heard him fall heavily on the turf, and without looking behind me, I galloped off to the other end of the field; there I turned around and saw my persecutor slowly rising from the ground and going into the stable. I stood under an oak tree and watched, but no one came to catch me. The time went on, the sun was very hot, the flies swarmed around me, and settled on my bleeding flanks where the spurs had dug in. I felt hungry, for I had not eaten since the early morning, but there was not enough grass in that meadow for a goose to live on. I wanted to lie down and rest, but with the saddle strapped tightly on, there was no comfort, and there was not a drop of water to drink. The afternoon wore on, and the sun got low. I saw the other cólts led in, and I knew they were having a good feed.

"At last, just as the sun went down, I saw the old master come out with a sieve in his hand. He was a very fine old gentleman with quite white hair, but his voice was what I should know him by among a thousand. It was not high, nor yet low, but full, and clear, and kind; and when he gave orders, it was so steady and decided, that everyone knew, both horses and men, that he expected to be obeyed. He came quietly along, now and then shaking the oats about that he had in the sieve, and speaking cheerfully and gently to me, 'Come along, lassie, come along, lassie; come along, come along.' I stood still and let him come up; he held the oats to me and I began to eat without fear; his voice took all my fear away. He stood by, patting and stroking me while I was eating, and seeing the clots of blood on my side, he seemed very vexed; 'Poor lassie! it was a bad business, a bad business!' then he quietly took the rein and led me back to the stable; just at the door stood Samson. I laid my ears back and snapped at him. 'Stand back,' said the master, 'and keep out of her way; you've done a bad day's work for this filly.' He growled out something about a vicious brute. 'Hark ye,' said the father, 'a bad-tempered man will never make a good-tempered horse. You've not learned your trade yet, Samson.' Then he led me into my box, took off the saddle and bridle with his own hands, and tied me up; then he called for a pail of warm water and a sponge, took off his coat, and while the stable man held the pail, he sponged my sides a good while so tenderly that I was sure he knew how sore and bruised they were. 'Whoa! my pretty one,' he said, 'stand still, stand still.' His very voice did me good, and the bathing was very comfortable. The skin was so broken at the corners of my mouth that I could not eat the hay, the stalks hurt me. He looked closely at it, shook his head, and told the man to fetch a good bran mash and put some meal into it. How good that mash was! and so soft and healing to my mouth. He stood by all the time I was eating, stroking me and talking to the man. 'If a high-mettled creature like this,' said he, 'can't be broken in by fair means, she will never be good for anything.'

"After that, he often came to see me, and when my mouth was healed, the other breaker, Job they called him, went on training me; he was steady and thoughtful, and I soon learned what he wanted."

THE GARDEN DISCOVERED

from
THE SECRET GARDEN
by
FRANCES HODGSON BURNETT

Mary Lennox is the heroine of The Secret Garden: *but heroine is not the word you feel like applying to her at the beginning of the book. She is a spoiled, sulky child, who has come from India to live at her uncle's home in Yorkshire, in England. Indeed, part of the pleasure of reading the early chapters of* The Secret Garden *lies in disliking Mary: and a part of the pleasure of the rest lies in slowly coming to like her very much. Her discovery of a locked and deserted garden within the bigger garden, her cultivation of it with a boy called Dickon, and their use of the garden to restore health to a supposed invalid, Mary's cousin, Colin—all these things*

help to change Mary from a horror to a bearable person. You'll need to know that Martha Sowerby is a country girl who teaches Mary to stand on her own feet, and that Mrs. Medlock is her uncle's housekeeper, and that English robins are much smaller than their American namesakes.

Frances Hodgson Burnett lived from 1849 to 1924: her most famous book was Little Lord Fauntleroy, *which became a sort of joke – Cedric its hero, became everybody's idea of a namby-pamby child: but it's a much better book than that.*

Mary felt lonelier than ever when she knew Martha was no longer in the house. She went out into the garden as quickly as possible, and the first thing she did was to run round and round the fountain flower garden ten times. She counted the times carefully, and when she had finished, she felt in better spirits. The sunshine made the whole place look different. The high, deep, blue sky arched over Misselthwaite, as well as over the moor, and she kept lifting her face and looking up into it, trying to imagine what it would be like to lie down on one of the little snow-white clouds and float about. She went into the first kitchen-garden and found Ben Weatherstaff working there with two other gardeners. The change in the weather seemed to have done him good. He spoke to her of his own accord.

"Springtime's coming," he said. "Cannot tha' smell it?"

Mary sniffed and thought she could.

"I smell something nice and fresh and damp," she said.

"That's th' good rich earth," he answered, digging away. "It's in a good humor makin' ready to grow things. It's glad when plantin' time comes. It's dull in th' winter when it's got nowt to do. In th' flower gardens out there, things will be stirrin' down below in th' dark. Th' sun's warmin' 'em. You'll see bits o' green spikes stickin' out o' th' black earth after a bit."

"What will they be?" asked Mary.

"Crocuses an' snowdrops an' daffydowndillys. Has tha' never seen them?"

"No. Everything is hot, and wet, and green after the rains in India," said Mary. "And I think things grow up in a night."

"These won't grow up in a night," said Weatherstaff. "Tha'll have to wait for 'em. They'll poke up a bit higher here, and push out a spike more there, an' uncurl a leaf this day an' another that. You watch 'em."

"I am going to," answered Mary.

Very soon, she heard the soft, rustling flight of wings again, and she knew at once that the robin had come again. He was very pert and lively, and hopped about so close to her feet, and put his head on one side and looked at her so shyly that she asked Ben Weatherstaff a question.

"Do you think he remembers me?" she said.

"Remembers thee!" said Weatherstaff indignantly. "He knows every cabbage stump in th' gardens, let alone th' people. He's never seen a little wench here before, an' he's bent on findin' out all about thee. Tha's no need to try to hide anything from *him*."

"Are things stirring down below in the dark in that garden where he lives?" Mary inquired.

"What garden?" grunted Weatherstaff, becoming surly again.

"The one where the old rose-trees are." She could not help asking, because she wanted so much to know. "Are all the flowers dead, or do some of them come again in the summer? Are there ever any roses?"

"Ask him," said Ben Weatherstaff, hunching his shoulders toward the robin. "He's the only one as knows. No one else has seen inside it for ten year'."

Ten years was a long time, Mary thought. She had been born ten years ago.

She walked away, slowly thinking. She had begun to like the garden, just as she had begun to like the robin and Dickon and Martha's mother. She was beginning to like Martha, too. That seemed a good many people to like – when you were not used to liking. She thought of the robin as one of the people. She went to her walk outside the long, ivy-covered wall over which she could see the treetops; and the second time she walked up and down, the most interesting and exciting thing happened to her, and it was all through Ben Weatherstaff's robin.

She heard a chirp and a twitter, and when she looked at the bare flowerbed at her left side, there he was hopping about and pretending to peck things out of the earth to persuade her that he had not followed her. But she knew he had followed her, and the surprise so filled her with delight that she almost trembled a little.

"You do remember me!" she cried. "You do! You are

prettier than anything else in the world!"

She chirped, and talked, and coaxed and he hopped and flirted his tail and twittered. It was as if he were talking. His red vest was like satin, and he puffed his tiny breast out and was so fine and so grand and so pretty that it was really as if he were showing her how important and like a human person a robin could be. Mistress Mary forgot that she had ever been contrary in her life when he allowed her to draw closer and closer to him, and bend down and talk and try to make something like robin sounds.

Oh! to think that he should actually let her come as near to him as that! He knew nothing in the world would make her put out her hand toward him or startle him in the least tiniest way. He knew it because he was a real person – only nicer than any other person in the world. She was so happy that she scarcely dared to breathe.

The flowerbed was not quite bare. It was bare of flowers because the perennial plants had been cut down for their winter rest, but there were tall shrubs and low ones which grew together at the back of the bed; and as the robin hopped about under them, she saw him hop over a small pile of freshly turned-up earth. He stopped on it to look for a worm. The earth had been turned up because a dog had been trying to dig up a mole, and he had scratched quite a deep hole.

Mary looked at it, not really knowing why the hole was there, and as she looked saw something almost buried in the newly turned soil. It was something like a ring of rusty iron or brass, and when the robin flew up into a tree near by, she put out her hand and picked the ring up. It was more than a ring, however; it was an old key which looked as if it had been buried a long time.

Mistress Mary stood up and looked at it with an almost frightened face as it hung from her finger.

"Perhaps it has been buried for ten years," she said in a whisper. "Perhaps it is the key to the garden!"

She looked at the key quite a long time. She turned it over and over, and thought about it. As I have said before, she was not a child who had been trained to ask permission or consult her elders about things. All she thought about the key was that, if it was the key to the closed garden, and she could find out where the door was, she could perhaps open it and see what was inside the walls, and what had happened to the old rose-trees. It was because it had been shut up so long that she wanted to see it. It seemed as if it must be different from other places and that something strange must have happened to it during ten years. Besides that, if she liked it, she could go into it every day and shut the door behind her, and she could make up some play of her own and play it quite alone, because nobody would ever know where she was, but would think the door was still locked and the key buried in the earth. The thought of that pleased her very much.

Living, as it were, all by herself in a house with a hundred mysteriously closed rooms and having nothing whatever to do to amuse herself, had set her inactive brain to work and was actually awakening her imagination. There is no doubt that the fresh, strong, pure air from the moor had a great deal to do with it. Just as it had given her an appetite, and fighting with the wind had stirred her blood, so the same things had stirred her mind. In India, she had always been too hot and languid and weak to care much about anything, but in this place she was beginning to care and to want to do new things. Already she felt less "contrary," though she did not know why.

She put the key in her pocket and walked up and down her walk. No one but herself ever seemed to come there, so she could walk slowly and look at the wall, or, rather, at the ivy growing on it. The ivy was the baffling thing. Howsoever carefully she looked, she could see nothing but thickly growing, glossy, dark green leaves. She was very much disappointed. Something of her contrariness came back to her as she paced the wall and looked over it at the tree-tops inside. It seemed so silly, she said to herself, to be near it and not be able to get in. She took the key in her pocket when she went back to the house, and she made up her mind that she would always carry it with her when she went out, so that if she ever should find the hidden door, she would be ready.

Mrs. Medlock had allowed Martha to sleep all night at the cottage, but she was back at her work in the morning with cheeks redder than ever and in the best of spirits.

"I got up at four o'clock," she said. "Eh! it was pretty on th' moor with th' birds gettin' up an' th' rabbits scamperin' about an' th' sun rising. I didn't walk all the way. A man gave me a ride in his cart, an' I can tell you I did enjoy myself."

She was full of stories of the delights of her day out. Her mother had been glad to see her, and they had got the baking and washing all out of the way. She had even made each of the children a dough-cake with a bit of brown sugar in it.

"I had 'em all pipin' hot when they came in from playin' on th' moor. An' th' cottage all smelt o' nice, clean, hot bakin' an' there was a good fire, an' they just shouted for joy. Our Dickon, he said our cottage was good enough for a king to live in."

In the evening, they had all sat around the fire, and Martha and her mother had sewed patches on torn clothes and mended stockings, and Martha had told them about the little girl who had come from India and who had been waited on all her life by what Martha called "blacks" until she didn't know how to put on her own stockings.

"Eh! they did like to hear about you," said Martha. "They wanted to know all about th' blacks an' about th' ship you came in. I couldn't tell 'em enough."

Mary reflected a little.

"I'll tell you a great deal more before your next day out," she said, "so that you will have more to talk about. I dare say they would like to hear about riding on elephants and camels, and about the officers going to hunt tigers."

"My word!" cried the delighted Martha, "It would set 'em clean off their heads. Would tha' really do that, Miss? It would be the same as a wild beast show like we heard they had in York once."

"India is quite different from Yorkshire," Mary said slowly, as she thought the matter over. "I never thought of that. Did Dickon and your mother like to hear you talk about me?"

"Why, our Dickon's eyes nearly started out o' his head, they got that round," answered Martha. "But Mother, she was put out about your seemin' to be all by yourself like. She said: 'Hasn't Mr. Craven got no governess for her, nor no nurse?' and I said: 'No, he hasn't, though Mrs. Medlock says he will when he thinks of it, but she says he mayn't think of it for two or three years.'"

"I don't want a governess," said Mary sharply.

"But Mother says you ought to be learnin' your book by this time an' you ought to have a woman to look after you, an' she says: 'Now Martha, you just think how you'd feel yourself, in a big place like that, wanderin' about alone, an' no mother. You do your best to cheer her up,' she says, an' I said I would."

Mary gave her a long, steady look.

"You do cheer me up," she said. "I like to hear you talk."

Presently, Martha went out of the room and came back with something held in her hands under her apron.

"What does tha' think," she said, with a cheerful grin. "I've brought thee a present."

"A present!" exclaimed Mistress Mary. How could a cottage full of fourteen hungry people give anyone a present!

"A man was drivin' across the moor peddlin'," Martha explained. "An' he stopped his cart at our door. He had pots an' pans an' odds an' ends, but Mother had no money to buy anythin'. Just as he was goin' away, our 'Lizbeth Ellen called out: 'Mother, he's got skippin'-ropes with red an' blue handles.' An' Mother, she calls out quite sudden: 'Here, stop, mister! How much are they?' An' he says 'Tuppence,' an' Mother she began fumblin' in her pocket, an' she says to me: 'Martha, tha's brought thee thy wages like a good lass, an' I've got four places to put every penny, but I'm just goin' to take tuppence out of it to buy that child a skippin'-rope,' an' she bought one, an' here it is."

She brought it out from under her apron and exhibited it quite proudly. It was a strong, slender rope with a striped red and blue handle at each end, but Mary Lennox had never seen a skipping-rope before. She gazed at it with a mystified expression.

"What is it for?" she asked curiously.

"For!" cried out Martha. "Does tha' mean that they've not got skippin'-ropes in India, for all they've got elephants and tigers and camels? This is what it's for; just watch me."

And she ran into the middle of the room and, taking a handle in each hand, began to skip, and skip, and skip, while Mary turned in her chair to stare at her, and the queer faces in the old portraits seemed to stare at her, too, and wonder what on earth this common little cottager had the impudence to be doing under their very noses. But Martha did not even see them. The interest and curiosity in Mistress Mary's face delighted her, and she went on skipping and counted as she skipped until she had reached a hundred.

"I could skip longer than that," she said when she stopped. "I've skipped as much as five hundred when I was twelve, but I wasn't as fat then as I am now, an' I was in practice."

Mary got up from her chair beginning to feel excited herself.

"It looks nice," she said. "Your mother is a kind woman. Do you think I could ever skip like that?"

"You just try it," urged Martha, handing her the skipping-rope. "You can't skip a hundred at first, but if you practice, you'll mount up. That's what Mother said. She says: 'Nothin' will do her more good than skippin'-rope. It's th' sensiblest toy a child can have. Let her play out in th' fresh air skippin', an' it'll stretch her legs an' arms an' give her some strength in 'em.'"

It was plain that there was not a great deal of strength in Mistress Mary's arms and legs when she first began to skip. She was not very clever at it, but she liked it so much that she did not want to stop.

"Put on tha' things and run an' skip out o' doors," said Martha. "Mother said I must tell you to keep out o' doors as much as you could, even when it rains a bit, so as tha' wrap up warm."

Mary put on her coat and hat and took her skipping-rope over her arm. She opened the door to go out, and then suddenly thought of something and turned back rather slowly.

"Martha," she said, "they were your wages. It was your twopence really. Thank you." She said it stiffly because she was not used to thanking people or noticing that they did things for her. "Thank you," she said, and held out her hand because she did not know what else to do.

Martha gave her hand a clumsy little shake, as if she was not accustomed to this sort of thing either. Then she laughed.

"Eh! tha' art a queer, old-womanish thing," she said. "If tha'd been our 'Lizabeth Ellen, tha'd have given me a kiss."

Mary looked stiffer than ever.

"Do you want me to kiss you?"

Martha laughed again.

"Nay, not me," she answered. "If tha' was different, p'raps tha'd want to thysel'. But tha' isn't. Run off outside an' play with thy rope."

Mistress Mary felt a little awkward as she went out of the room. Yorkshire people seemed strange, and Martha was always rather a puzzle to her. At first, she had disliked her very much, but now she did not.

The skipping-rope was a wonderful thing. She counted and skipped, and skipped and counted, until her cheeks were quite red, and she was more interested than she had ever been since she was born. The sun was shining, and a little wind was blowing – not a rough wind, but one which came in delightful little gusts and brought a fresh scent of newly turned earth with it. She skipped around the fountain garden, and up one walk and down another. She skipped at last into the kitchen-garden and saw Ben Weatherstaff digging and talking to his robin, which was hopping about him. She skipped down the walk toward him, and he lifted his head and looked at her with a curious expression. She had wondered if he would notice her. She really wanted him to see her skip.

"Well!" he exclaimed. "Upon my word! P'raps tha' art a young 'un, after all, an' p'raps tha's got child's blood in thy veins instead of sour buttermilk. Tha's skipped red into thy cheeks as sure as my name's Ben Weatherstaff. I wouldn't have believed tha' could do it."

"I never skipped before," Mary said. "I'm just beginning. I can only go up to twenty."

"Tha' keep on," said Ben. "Tha' shapes well enough at it for a young 'un that's lived with heathen. Just see how he's watchin' thee," jerking his head toward the robin. "He followed after thee yesterday. He'll be at it again today. He'll be bound to find out what th' skippin'-rope is. He's never seen one. Eh!" shaking his head at the bird, "tha' curiosity will be the death of thee some time if tha' doesn't look sharp."

Mary skipped around all the gardens and around the orchard, resting every few minutes. At length, she went to her own special walk and made up her mind to try if she could skip the whole length of it. It was a good long skip, and she began slowly, but before she had gone halfway down the path, she was so hot and breathless that she was obliged to stop. She did not mind much, because she had already counted up to thirty. She stopped with a little laugh of pleasure, and there, lo and behold, was the robin swaying on a long branch of ivy. He had followed her, and he greeted her with a chirp. As Mary had skipped toward him, she felt something heavy in her pocket strike against her at each jump; and when she saw the robin, she laughed again.

"You showed me where the key was yesterday," she said. "You ought to show me the door today; but I don't believe you know!"

The robin flew from his swinging spray of ivy onto the top of the wall, and he opened his beak and sang a loud, lovely trill, merely to show off. Nothing in the world is quite as adorably lovely as a robin when he shows off – and they are nearly always doing it.

Mary Lennox had heard a great deal about Magic in her Ayah's stories, and she always said what happened almost at that moment was Magic.

One of the nice little gusts of wind rushed down the walk, and it was a stronger one than the rest. It was strong enough to wave the branches of the trees, and it was more than strong enough to sway the trailing sprays of untrimmed ivy hanging from the wall. Mary had stepped close to the robin, and suddenly the gust of wind swung aside some loose ivy trails, and more suddenly still she jumped toward it and caught it in her hand. This she did because she had seen something under it – a round knob which had been covered by the leaves hanging over it. It was the knob of a door.

She put her hands under the leaves and began to pull and push them aside. Thick as the ivy hung, it nearly all was a loose and swinging curtain, though some had crept over wood and iron. Mary's heart began to thump and her hands to shake a little in her delight and excitement. The robin kept singing and twittering away and tilting his head on one side, as if he were as excited as she was. What was this under her hands which was square and made of iron and which her fingers found a hole in?

It was the lock of the door which had been closed ten years, and she put her hand in her pocket, drew out the key, and found it fitted the keyhole. She put the key in and turned it. It took two hands to do it, but it did turn.

And then she took a long breath and looked behind her up the long walk to see if anyone was coming. No one was coming. No one ever did come, it seemed, and she took another long breath, because she could not help it, and she held back the swinging curtain of ivy and pushed back the door which opened slowly – slowly.

Then she slipped through it, and shut it behind her, and stood with her back against it, looking about her and breathing quite fast with excitement, and wonder, and delight.

She was standing *inside* the secret garden.

Word Guide

acrid: burning taste or smell

apothecary: (a-POTH-e-kerry) a druggist: someone who sold medical drugs

Ayah: (EYE-a) a children's nurse or maidservant in India

bauble: trinket

bed curtains: drapes hung around a bed for warmth

boater: a straw hat

bows: the front of a ship

breaking in: training a horse to accept a harness and be ridden

bulwark: (BULL-werk) the side of a ship, above deck level – but in *Moonfleet*, bulwark means a natural screen

calliope: (ka-LI-o-pee) a musical steam instrument featured at fairs and circuses

canted: leaned over

capstan: a device on a ship's deck for winding up cable or rope

catspaw: a light breeze

chanterelles: (shan't-e-rels) a kind of mushroom

charnel: place where dead bodies or bones are kept

chevy: (CHEV-ee) a game of chase; those caught were held prisoner

choler: (COLL-er) anger

cob: see **roan cob**

cognizance: knowledge, awareness

collar: part of a horse's harness, around its neck

comforter: a wool scarf

companion: a ladder or stairway from the deck down to a ship's cabin

court-plaster: bandage, adhesive tape

coxswain: (COCK-sun) someone who steers a ship

cross-trees: timber beams across the mast

diatribe: bitter criticism

dirk: (derk) a long dagger

dot-and-carry: limpingly

drawing-room: formal parlor; living room

ensign: (EN-sun) a ship's flag

environed: surrounded, held

Eton jackets: boys' short black coats, first worn at Eton School

excisemen: those responsible for collecting excise (tax on certain goods) and preventing smugglers from evading the tax by bringing in goods from abroad

fancied: imagined

felons: criminals

ferule: a stick used for punishment

forecastle: (FOK-sel) the forward section of a ship, with living quarters and storage space

forelock: the lock of hair over a horse's forehead

gallery: a passageway

guillemots: (GILL-ee-mots) diving birds, of the auk family

halberds: ancient weapons, combining spears and axeheads

hammer: the part of a pistol that strikes and ignites the gunpowder

hash: see **settling his hash**

helm: the tiller that steers a ship

inanition: emptiness

Inquisition: medieval church court which tortured and killed non-believers

junk: lump of chewing tobacco

kitchen-garden: vegetable garden

lander: a smuggler

lay to: to bring a ship to a standstill without anchoring, by pointing the ship toward the wind and adjusting the sails

larboard: (LAR-berd) the left-hand side of a ship

leeward: (LOO-erd) the direction from which the wind is coming

lethargy: a state of tiredness, lacking in energy

line: a rope or cable

luff: to sail a ship close to the wind

luster: brilliant light, shining radiance

matchlock: a gun

mill-race: a current of water turning a millwheel

minions: servile followers

missed stays: a ship was said to have missed stays when it failed to go about (change direction). Israel Hands uses the expression to mean he himself is in trouble.

mizzen shrouds: in a three-masted vessel like the *Hispaniola*, the mizzen was the rearmost of the masts and sails. The shrouds were sets of ropes from the masthead to the sides of the ship supporting the mast.

moiety: a portion, share

moor: a heath

niche: a recessed space

Pachyderm: (PAK-ee-derm) a thick-skinned mammal, especially an elephant or a rhinoceros

paddock: a small, enclosed field for horses

palatable: tasty, agreeable

peremptory: decisive, absolute

pertinacity stubbornness, tenacity

pettifogging: quibbling

pinchbeck: fake

plethoric: over-full

pomatum: (po-MAY-tum) a scented ointment for hair

port scuppers: port is the left-hand side of the vessel, and scuppers are holes in a ship's side for draining water from the deck

potting-shed: special area for transplanting seedlings into pots

priming: gunpowder

propitiatory: bringing good luck

puncheon: (PUN-shun) a large cask, but also a liquid measure of between 75 and 100 gallons: a lot of water!

quid: a lump of tobacco, for chewing

ravenous: very hungry

reconnoiter: survey, examine, check out

recusant: person who refuses to submit or comply

ribands: ribbons

roan cob: a cob is a strong, short-legged horse, and a roan is a dark or bay or chestnut-colored horse with flecks of gray or white

scimitar: curved sword

scuppers: see **port scuppers**

scythe: a curved blade on a long handle, for cutting grass or grain

serge: strong ribbed fabric

settling his hash: killing someone

shrouds: see **mizzen shrouds**

spinney: a small wood

starboard: (STAR-berd) the right-hand side of a ship

stays: see **missed stays**

stem on: the stem is the front of a ship, so that to run stem on is to sail straight ahead

stern: the back of a ship

subaltern: (SUB-ul-tern) a junior officer

surcingle: strong strap, used to hold a saddle on a horse

surreptitiously: secretively, slyly

sward: grassy patch of ground

ulster: a rough, baggy kind of overcoat, first sold in Belfast, Northern Ireland (Ulster)

Ultima Thule: the most distant goal of human endeavor

velocity: speed

viand: food, especially meat

voracity: greed

warder: prison guard

weaned: a young mammal is weaned when it learns to take food other than its mother's milk

went about: a ship "goes about" when it changes course

younker: youngster

ACKNOWLEDGMENTS

The compiler and publishers gratefully acknowledge permission to reproduce the following copyright material:

"Under the Hill" from THE HOBBIT by J. R. R. Tolkien. Copyright © 1966 by J. R. R. Tolkien. Reprinted by permission of Houghton Mifflin Company and HarperCollins Publishers Inc., all rights reserved.
Excerpt from THE BORROWERS by Mary Norton. Copyright © 1953, 1952 and renewed 1981, 1980 by Mary Norton, Beth Krush, and Joe Krush, reprinted by permission of Harcourt Brace & Company.
"The Invisible Child" from TALES FROM MOOMIN VALLEY by Tove Jansson © Tove Jansson 1962, by permission of A&C Black (Publishers) Ltd.
"Who'll Teach Smith to Read?" from SMITH by Leon Garfield © Leon Garfield 1967, by permission of John Johnson (Author's Agent) Ltd.
"Through the Door" © Oxford University Press 1958. Reprinted from TOM'S MIDNIGHT GARDEN by Philippa Pearce (1958) by permission of Oxford University Press.
"Wilbur's Escape" C. J. White 1952. Reprinted from CHARLOTTE'S WEB by E. B. White by permission of HarperCollins Publishers Inc.

While every effort has been made to obtain permission, there may still be cases in which we have failed to trace a copyright holder, and we would like to apologize for any apparent negligence.